MENACE

at the
Marina

AN ALEX PAIGE MYSTERY
BOOK 6

THERESA L CARTER

Contents

Chapter 1

"You're not going to kill us."

Alex scowled at the instructor. "I'm not sure I believe you."

"We've got a nine-hundred pound keel beneath us," he explained. His patience made it obvious she wasn't the first student to receive this explanation. "It is physically impossible for us to tip over."

She squinted at the whitecaps forming on the lake beyond the harbor. "You positive about that?"

William grinned at her from the bow. "This is a first."

"What?"

"You, scared."

"I'm not scared."

"Suuure. And I'm not getting married this weekend."

Alex grinned. "You're getting married this weekend!" she squealed. It had been the exact right thing to say to ease her fears. Sailing had always intrigued her, but she never seriously considered learning. But, when William asked Alex if she'd take a sailing lesson with him the week of his wedding to Billy, she had to say yes. He wanted to surprise his fiancé, who was an avid sailor, by showing interest in his hobby. Alex gripped the tiller and faced Garrett, their instructor. "You're sure I won't kill us?"

Garrett shook his head and drew his finger across his life vest. "Cross my heart and hope to–not–die," he winked. "You're perfectly safe. I promise. Now, see how that jib is flapping? You want to push the rudder just a bit until it flies straight." She followed his instructions. "Great!"

As the small boat headed in a straight line out to the vast expanse of Lake Michigan, Alex grinned like a tween who'd just gotten Taylor Swift tickets. Her fear disappeared, and she reveled in the water's nearness, so close she could stick her hand out of the boat and drag it in the waves. As someone who loved being on the water and adored being near it so much she'd bought a condo in Chicago that overlooked the same lake, her hesitation to sail had surprised her. Alex wasn't fearless; she'd been through cancer, among other things, and knew enough to have a healthy dose of flight in her system, but she also had a heaping serving of fight. When things scared her, instead of backing down, she dealt with them head on.

"That's my girl," William said. The two were so close it often seemed like they could read each other's minds.

They spent the next hour and a half becoming more and more comfortable with sailing the small vessel. Their instructor had them switch places, ensuring they each got to experience the different tasks involved. It was a windy, cloudy day, and though some sailboats were on the lake, most of them were still docked, waiting for nicer weather.

"You're taking more lessons this week, right?" Alex asked.

William nodded. He sat comfortably in the stern, casually nudging the rudder to make adjustments. "Yes. I wanted to get at least two more in before Saturday. Fortunately, I've also got an assignment to write about it, so it's all covered."

"And you accuse me of being a workaholic," Alex said. While they were both travel writers, their paths were very different. William wrote for traditional outlets as a freelancer; Alex's primary outlet was her website, WellTraveledPaige.com.

"Like you don't have interviews and story ideas lined up," William accused.

Alex grinned, albeit a bit sheepishly. "Got me."

They neared the harbor and Garrett took over, so William scooted closer to her. "What's up for you?" he asked. "I'm sure you've got something set up at the art center."

"And the preserve," she nodded. They were in Sheboygan, Wisconsin, and with her passion for the arts, there was no way Alex would miss an opportunity to see the John Michael Kohler Arts Center and the Kohler Arts Preserve, which had just opened that summer. "Supposedly there's an artist who built sculptures out of chicken bones."

William laughed. "Ew. But also, cool. That's something I'd like to see."

"Too bad you'll be so busy this week, you know, getting ready for your wedding." Alex grinned as she accepted Garrett's hand and jumped onto the dock. "Speaking of which, what's on deck," she winked, "for today?"

The sailing instructor shook his head, chuckling slightly at Alex's lame joke, and William groaned. "Don't quit your day job. We're having lunch at the resort. Trying dishes for Saturday."

The two friends thanked Garrett and walked up the pier. "I still can't believe you've pulled this together so quickly. You just proposed three months ago."

"Three and a half. Plenty of time. Besides, it's a small wedding, and I'm used to planning cross-country road trips. I can handle a little get together."

William had said it lightly, but Alex could sense the underlying tension. She knew he wanted this weekend to go perfectly. She stopped him and made him face her. "No matter what, it's going to be beautiful and you get to marry the love of your life."

He grinned. "Promise me one thing."

"Anything."

"No dead bodies this time. Deal?"

Alex pasted a smile on her face. In the last year, they'd encountered so many murders she felt like she was back at her old job as an investigative reporter. Each case had been an instance of being in the wrong place at the wrong time. At least everyone had gotten what was coming to them. "Deal."

They continued walking. "Speaking of dead bodies," William began, "do you know when Cassidy and Reid are getting here?"

Alex guffawed. "What? They're archaeologists. They deal with dead bodies all the time."

"I guess that's one way to put it." They stopped at the end of the sidewalk, where one path led to the parking lot and the other to the yacht club. "As a matter of fact, I'm meeting them right now. They're also doing double-duty this week."

"Oh?"

"Yeah. She didn't tell me much, but said there's been an interesting find at the marine sanctuary. I'm sure I'll find out more at lunch."

"Tell them I said hi and thank them for coming."

"I will, but you can thank them yourself tonight."

"That's right. I forgot we'd planned dinner."

"You've had a few things on your mind. I'll see you in a few hours." Alex leaned in to give William a hug and kissed him on the cheek. He headed towards the lot and she walked in the other direction, towards the club. She fairly bounced. The morning's lesson had started out a bit shaky, and Alex was a little mad at herself for being afraid. *But,* she reminded herself, *you beat that. You got through it. That's what you do.* She grinned. *Yep, that is exactly what I do.*

Alex pulled open the heavy door which, predictably, had a ship's wheel hanging on the outside. She entered a low-ceilinged hallway; the interior felt like an English pub, dominated by dark woods and accented with burgundies and deep blues until she got past the entry. Then it opened up to a bright space decorated in pastels and whites. There was no mistaking it was a yacht club, however, with all the rope and mermaid motifs sprinkled about the place. That, and the wall of windows overlooking the marina.

The sky had cleared, and there were patches of blue and picturesque puffy clouds. Sailboats—the big vessels, not the tiny boat she'd been on—bobbed in the water in between speed boats and yachts. Even though she'd just gotten back to land, Alex yearned to be back out on the water, this time simply enjoying herself, preferably with a cocktail in hand while someone else did the heavy work of sailing.

As she scanned the boats, she saw her friend sitting at a table outside. Cassidy's long, blonde hair and tan figure were hard to miss. The striking woman leaned back, her eyes closed. A slight breeze picked up strands of her hair, teasing them around her face. As Alex approached the table, Cassidy turned her head and opened her eyes, her face brightening with her smile. Her incisors were a tad long, giving her an almost feral look. She stood up, and Alex was once again amazed at the fluidity of her movements and the strength behind them. They hugged tightly.

"Sit, sit," Cassidy said, and Alex took the seat next to her so she could also face the docks. Cassidy ran her fingers through Alex's curls. "Look how long your hair's gotten! And so thick and soft. Was it always curly?"

Alex grinned, running her own fingers through her hair. "Yes, but it's come back thicker, believe it or not."

Cassidy leaned over and wrapped a curl around her finger. When she released it, it bounced like a spring. "Lovely. I heard hair changes after chemo. That must have been worrisome."

Alex shrugged. "I'm just glad to have hair again. But enough about me. You look fantastic. Of course. And speaking of looking fantastic, where's that handsome Reid?"

"He's diving. I couldn't tear him away this morning." Cassidy browsed the menu. "Want to start off with cheese curds?"

"When in Wisconsin," Alex said.

Cassidy motioned for the server. She ordered their appetizer and a bottle of Fumé Blanc. After the server left, Cassidy leaned back. "Actually, I told him I wanted some girl time and he could meet up with us later."

"I'll never say no to seeing Reid, but good call. So, you mentioned you're working this week?"

Cassidy nodded. "You know this whole coastline's now a marine sanctuary, right?"

Alex nodded. "Yes, to protect all those shipwrecks. What are there, thirty-six?"

"More than that, but there are that many on the National Register. The water's cold enough they're preserved really well. Honestly, I'm surprised they made it happen. That's a whole lot of shoreline and area to coordinate."

The server approached with their wine. She poured the two women their glasses and left, so Alex replied. "Good thing Trevor Kaine's no longer around. He'd be trying to destroy it."

"Trevor Kaine?" Cassidy asked. She took a sip of her wine. "Ah. Nothing like a crisp white on a beautiful day with a beautiful friend."

They touched glasses. After Alex took a small drink, she explained. "It's a long story, but he was a Chicago developer–developer being generous, since he mostly destroyed things–who tried to take over a lovely resort and a nature preserve in Door County."

"Tried?"

Alex nodded. "Let's just say he had an untimely demise."

Cassidy's eyes cleared with recognition, and she snapped her fingers. "He's the one who fell off the overlook, right?"

Alex shivered at the memory. "Couldn't have happened to a nicer man. Sorry. I shouldn't have said that." She still sometimes woke up from nightmares, her subconscious reliving the scene. She cleared her throat and decided to think about happier things. "That trip is when William met Billy."

Cassidy beamed. "Ah, the two lovebirds. I'm excited to meet Billy. So what happened to the resort and preserve?"

"Still around. The resort had been in Evelyn Dahl's family for generations. You'll get to meet her; she's coming to the wedding."

"So it seems we're not the only friends you've met through less than ideal circumstances."

"There do seem to have been a lot of those," Alex said, ruefully. "At least something good's come out of them. A lot of something goods." She smiled, then changed subjects. "I didn't think shipwrecks were your thing."

"It depends on the shipwreck," Cassidy said. "If there's a tie back to any Indigenous people, then yes; for example, many of the Spanish ships in the Caribbean. That's why we learned to dive, actually. We didn't want to be limited to just the finds that were on dry land."

"I thought most of the shipwrecks around here were from the 1800s, and that they were mostly merchant ships."

"Mostly, yes, but Europeans weren't the first to navigate these waters."

"Ah, so you're looking for evidence of watercraft used by the First Peoples."

"Among other things." Cassidy's eyes shifted to focus above Alex's shoulder, and her face lit up. Alex turned to see Reid approaching, his stride powerful and graceful. She stood up as he neared and hugged him. He squeezed her tightly, but she could feel something was off. "This is a pleasant surprise," she said. "Cass told me you were out diving."

"I was." He remained standing and focused on his partner.

"Did you find something?" Cassidy asked.

Reid nodded, his face grim. "That's why I returned early. Sorry to intrude on your time together," he said to Alex, then turned back to Cassidy. "You'll want to see this."

Chapter 2

Cassidy gestured to her wineglass. "I can't dive for a few hours. You took pictures?"

"Of course. And video. I hate to tear you away, but this is important."

Alex studied Reid. His stiff posture, and that he hadn't sat down, told her he was anxious to show Cassidy whatever it was he'd found. He was tightly coiled, poised to leap at any moment. Alex reached over and squeezed her friend's hand. "Go. We'll catch up tonight. I've got some writing to do anyway."

"You're sure?" Cass said, while pushing her chair back.

"Positive. I want to capture this morning's adventure while it's still fresh," Alex said, tapping her temple. Her friends thanked her. Instead of walking back through the club, they strode down the dock to a large catamaran. Alex watched as Reid waited while Cassidy jumped on board, only slightly envious of their smooth grace. There was still a little wine in the bottle, so she poured it into her glass and then pulled her journal out of her bag. She wanted to record the sensations from her sailing lesson: the way the small boat jarred her body as it rhythmically hit wave after wave. The sound of the sails flapping like chattering magpies until they moved them in the right direction. The feel of the spray on her face, and the thrill of fear when she leaned back and knew her head was inches from the water. It was exhilarating, and Alex was envious that William would be going out again before the week was through. He was also getting married, and that was something that definitely did not make Alex envious. Ever since breaking up with Ben a year and a half before, she'd reveled in her solitude, and in learning who she could be when she wasn't told who she should be by someone else. She knew all relationships weren't like that; she thought of Cassidy and Reid, and William and Billy, for example, but that had been her most recent experience and she wasn't keen to take another chance anytime soon.

Alex shook her head. While she'd broken up with Ben a long time ago, he was still in her life, whether she wanted him to be or not. He kept showing up. He was there in Door County when William and Billy met, supposedly covering a story about Trevor Kaine's proposed development. Just a few months ago, he'd appeared in Billings, Montana. Alex had been there to attend and speak at a travel writing conference, and Ben claimed he'd switched his beat from investigative reporting to travel. Alex didn't buy it; she thought he was stalking her, and William agreed. She found out later he really was there to work, but it was to investigate rumors of corruption surrounding a retired billionaire and his plans to create a cult-like getaway.

Knowing he hadn't been there only because of her had eased her concerns a little, but she also thought it was awfully convenient that he kept getting assigned to places she'd be. Although she'd blocked him from all her social media accounts, travel was her job, and she couldn't exactly keep her destinations hidden.

Alex tried to shake these thoughts from her mind. It was going to be a wonderful week with friends converging on Sheboygan to celebrate William and Billy. Thinking of them made Alex imagine their marriage certificate, which would most likely show that William and William were the groom and groom, and she giggled.

She smelled his cologne before she heard him. "Sitting alone and laughing by yourself, eh? Should we be worried?"

Alex concentrated on not displaying any physical reaction. She realized she'd expected him to appear. Sheboygan was only two and a half hours from Chicago, and that was nothing for someone who'd travel across the country for a story. She closed her eyes and inhaled deeply through her nose, immediately realizing that was a mistake as his signature scent blasted her olfactory senses. She'd always hated that cologne. Cloying. Obnoxious. Invasive. Just like him.

She opened her eyes, then turned them to her ex. "Hello, Ben."

"You don't seem surprised to see me."

"I'm not."

"May I sit?"

"Might as well."

Ben pulled out the chair across from her. *At least he had the good sense not to sit next to me*, she thought. But she also realized he did it so he could study her reactions straight on. She played the game, focusing on him and waiting.

"You look good."

"I know."

Ben smiled, shaking his head. "So different from the Alex I knew."

She waited.

He cleared his throat. "This is quite the coincidence. Running into you here, I mean."

"I doubt that."

Ben narrowed his eyes. "You really are full of yourself, aren't you?"

Alex didn't dignify his question with an answer. She kept her eyes on him while reaching for her glass and bringing it to her lips. Ben was here for a reason, and while she wanted to rush things along so he'd leave, she also had no interest in engaging with him. She couldn't bring herself to act like this was a normal interaction, to have a conversation like she would with anyone else. That had never been easy with Ben, and it was impossible now.

"You know I know what you're doing. Stay silent and I'll fill the vacuum, because we humans abhor vacuums."

The corner of Alex's mouth upturned ever so slightly. She set her glass on the table, leaned back, and waited.

"I'm not here because of you," he protested.

"Great."

"God, you're infuriating. I'm here for a story, just like I was in Montana. I said it then and I'll say it now: it's not always about you, Alex Paige."

"Fantastic. Since you've got a story to cover, I won't keep you." She opened her journal to a blank page, knowing Ben would try to read anything she'd written, and picked up her pen.

"Don't you want to know what the story is? It's fascinating. Something you'd definitely be interested in."

Alex sighed. She knew the only way to get this over with was to let him say what he wanted to say. She considered getting up and walking away, but knew he'd just follow her. "Fine. Please, tell me, Ben. What is this fascinating story you just happen to be covering in Sheboygan, coincidentally, at the same time I'm in Sheboygan?"

"'Just happen to be' and 'coincidentally'—Alex Paige, being redundant? I can tell I'm getting under your skin."

She'd had enough. Alex pushed out her chair, grabbed her journal and pen and shoved them into her bag, and walked away without looking back. She could hear him laughing softly and she cursed herself. She knew better than to let him see he'd "gotten under her skin," as he put it.

Alex intercepted the server, who was coming out with a basket of cheese curds. She opened her purse and extracted a credit card. "I'm sorry, but we both had to leave."

The server waved off the payment. "Your friend took care of it. They've got a tab."

Alex nodded, putting her card away. "Feel free to eat those, if you'd like."

"You don't want them boxed up? Or to leave them with the gentleman at your table?"

Alex snorted. "He's no gentleman. If I didn't know it would get you in trouble, I'd tell you to dump them on his head."

The server laughed. "Got it. Well, I hope to see you and your friend again."

Alex resumed walking. She passed Cassidy and Reid sitting on the deck of their catamaran and considered joining them, but they were intently focused on a laptop and didn't raise their heads. Besides, she didn't want to give Ben any more insight into her life. The more people he could connect to her, the more angles he'd have to find out where she was and what she was doing.

She reached the corner of the yacht club and turned right, picking up her pace as she neared her car. Her breathing had increased along with her steps, and she was practically panting by the time she was safely inside her car. She leaned back, closing her eyes again, forcing herself to breathe slowly and calm down. A knock on the glass startled her, even though it shouldn't have.

Ben stood outside her door, motioning for her to roll down her window.

Alex ignored him, backing out and driving away. She refused to look in the rear-view mirror. She knew he'd be watching her, and that's the last thing she wanted to see. Her phone buzzed. A message on the screen of her dashboard let her know she'd gotten a text message and asked if she wanted to play it. She didn't recognize the number. She jabbed at the option that said No. But she kept glancing at her phone, and when she stopped at a red light, she pulled up the message.

You can't run from me forever, Alex. I'll always find you.

Alex shuddered. She'd blocked him. He must have gotten a new number. William was right. When Ben had shown up in Billings, William had warned her that her ex was a full-on stalker and he was becoming increasingly concerned about her safety. But Alex had been home the last few months, catching up on writing assignments. Ben knew where she lived and he hadn't shown up once. Well, only once. She had just begun to believe he was finally out of her life, and now this. He was here. In Sheboygan. It couldn't be a coincidence. She just knew it.

She shook her head to clear her thoughts. Her instinct was to call William, but this was his wedding week. There's no way she would burden him with her fears. Maybe she should call Emily. Alex was about to do so when she noticed the time. Her friend would be finishing up after the lunch rush and would soon be prepping for dinner. Emily's Lincoln Park restaurant, Elements, was one of the best places to eat in Chicago and was busy from the moment it opened until close. Besides, she knew Emily; she'd drop everything and drive up, then hunt for Ben and threaten him. Emily may be tiny, but she was one of the fiercest human beings

Alex knew, and when she was angry—nobody wanted to be on the receiving end of that, let alone a coward like her ex.

Alex pulled into the parking lot of Blue Harbor Resort, where the wedding party and guests would be staying. She looked around before getting out, half expecting Ben to be waiting for her, standing and staring like some horror movie villain. The coast was clear. Instead of going through the lobby, she entered through the door closest to her room, which was on the ground floor. While normally she preferred to be on higher floors, when she stayed at Blue Harbor she loved having a sliding glass door that let her walk across the grass straight to the shore. Alex dropped her bag on the wet bar, exchanged her tennies for sandals, and walked outside. She'd only walked a few feet when she stopped and cursed. She couldn't leave her sliding glass door unlocked, not with Ben around. Darn him, she muttered. Alex trudged back into her room, flipped the latch, and exited into the hallway, making sure she'd locked the door behind her.

Chapter 3

Alex buried her toes in the sand. She luxuriated in the feel of the cold smooth grains covering her feet. She tilted her face up to the late October sun, closing her eyes and listening to the calls of seagulls and the laughter of children. Rolling waves gently lapped the shore. From the sound alone, it was hard to believe she was in Wisconsin, but she knew Sheboygan was the freshwater surfing capital of the world. People came from all over to catch the waves in the Malibu of the Midwest. Unlike the California spot, they braved the water in fall and winter. She thought of a photo she'd seen of a man whose beard had become one huge icicle and shivered.

Today, the weather was fairly balmy. The breeze was strong enough for windsurfers, who glided over the water with sails, but it was too calm for traditional surfers riding on waves alone. After her encounter, what Alex really wanted to do was grab a drink from the bar and sit outside all afternoon, but she had someplace she wanted to see, and if she didn't do it this afternoon, she might not get the chance.

She'd hoped the balm of the breeze, the beach, and the water would ease her tension, but she kept picturing Ben as he approached her at the table, then at her car window, and for the first time since she'd broken up with him, she felt real fear.

The man had shown up when she was on assignment in Door County, he'd finagled his own assignment in Montana when he knew she'd be speaking at a conference there, and now he was here, in Sheboygan, the same week she was there for William's wedding. None of this was coincidence.

Alex straightened. *No*, she said to herself, *I refuse to let him control me. He did that long enough*. Determined, she strode back towards the resort. Despite her personal concerns, she had to smile as she took in the beautiful white building with its red-tiled roof. It reminded her of Hotel Coronado in California or the Grand Hotel in Mackinac Island, although she'd never been to the latter. A bucket list item, she thought. *Maybe after the wedding I'll drive north instead of back to Chicago.* As a travel writer, she could. Nobody waited for her back home, except for Ernie, her six-toed cat, but Emily wouldn't mind taking care of him a little longer. Alex smiled to herself as she thought of her fuchsia-topped friend. She'd barely seen her the last few months, even though their condos were next door to each other. What with her travel and with Emily's restaurant, they were both so busy they had to steal a few minutes for coffee on their balconies whenever they happened to be home at the same time.

I'm being silly, Alex thought. *Ben isn't dangerous. He's creepy, but he'd never hurt me.*

She rattled her head to shake the negative thoughts. Because Alex could never visit a place and *not* write about it, she'd planned an afternoon of exploring. First stop: a sculpture garden in the woods, and then the Indian Mounds. The two were within a couple of miles of each other. She didn't know why, but mound cultures, especially the effigy mound builders, had always fascinated her. Actually, she did know why: it was because so little was known about them, but the mounds were ubiquitous in the Midwest. Her innate curiosity drove her to learn more. Who were these people? Why did they build mounds? How did they build them with such precision?

A thought flashed. Cassidy might know. Telling the stories of indigenous peoples was hers and Reid's specialty, and they were actually here. Alex pulled out her phone, hesitating slightly. Reid had found something that concerned him and she didn't know if she should disturb them. *Can't hurt to ask*, she thought, and called.

Alex pulled into a small lot shaded by trees and parked in front of a large historical marker. She got out and walked towards the sign, followed closely by Cassidy. The other woman leaned in close to read how a local garden club had raised the money to buy the land to protect the mounds from being destroyed as so many others had been. "A garden club. I knew the story, but it's still crazy to think about."

"Isn't it? Hard to believe they were able to save this place."

"They did it a few dollars at a time. Reid is always saying little actions taken consistently can carve canyons, move mountains, and build cities."

"Who knew he was so wise?"

Cassidy grinned. "Don't tell him that. He'll be insufferable."

"He's already insufferably attractive. Speaking of Reid, he seemed pretty focused earlier. I'm surprised you could get away."

"Like he could stop me from seeing this, and from spending time with you. Not that he'd want to. He thinks you're amazing."

"Feeling's mutual. For you, too." They began walking the trail, the crunch of leaves underfoot barely heard over a buzzing chainsaw. Ranch homes bordered one edge of the park and a man in a plaid flannel jacket was cutting logs into firewood. He ignored the women.

"Besides, what he found earlier may shed some light on these," Cassidy said, sweeping her arm to encompass the park.

Alex had stopped in front of a sign indicating the small hill in front of her hadn't occurred naturally, but had been constructed. She raised her eyes to take in the surrounding woods. She counted at least ten more of these structures with that quick glance. It was odd to think of them as man-made, especially since trees grew out of most of them.

"Over a thousand years," Cassidy said with awe, "somebody made these over a thousand years ago. It's hard to fathom. Who were they? Why? And why so many?"

"If anybody can find out, it's you."

Cassidy gave her a small smile, shaking her head. "I appreciate the confidence, but their secrets have been buried for millennia."

"But Reid found something that may shed some light?"

Cassidy practically hummed with excitement. "We need to get more time with the ROV, but maybe."

"ROV?"

"Remote Operated Vehicle. The water's too deep for diving, so that's the only way we can see what's down there."

"How'd you find out about it, whatever 'it' is?" Alex asked, hoping Cassidy would be more forthcoming.

"Reid's friends with a consultant who's working with the sanctuary. They were checking out one of the shipwrecks and came across, as the director called it, an anomaly." Cassidy stopped and put her hands on her hips, surveying the terrain.

"You're really not going to tell me any more, are you?" Alex teased.

"Nope." Cassidy mimed locking her lips and throwing away the key. "I know you can get a confession out of a priest, but we're not saying anything until we have a better idea. Not that I don't trust you," she blurted.

Alex smiled and patted her friend on the shoulder. "I suppose I'll let it go, for now," she winked.

Cassidy grinned back. They resumed walking, stopping at each sign denoting which mound was a puma, a deer, or other effigy. They reached the edge of the parking lot. "Well, this was amazing. Thanks for calling me."

"Of course." Alex checked the time on her phone. "Are you still coming to dinner tonight?"

Cassidy nodded. "Wouldn't miss it. I'm just hoping I can drag Reid away from his research." They reached the parking lot and she paused to survey the park again. "A thousand years. He's definitely going to want to see this."

Alex walked down a brick-lined alley hung with Edison lights. She neared the sidewalk and could smell bacon before she turned the corner. As soon as she did, she heard tapping on the window of the restaurant where she was meeting her friends. William waved vigorously, and Billy sat next to him, grinning. She sped up and entered the restaurant, bypassing the waiting hostess. "Well, look who I found—it's the groom and the groom!"

Billy stood and hugged Alex tightly, surprising her. He was normally much more reserved. He was definitely more reserved than his fiancé.

"Don't hog all the hugs," William said.

Billy peered over her shoulder at his partner. "Shh. You get to see her all the time."

"Not all the time."

"More often than I do. I had to go to North Carolina to see you last," he said to Alex.

She smiled. The last time she'd seen Billy, they'd been in Asheville to celebrate a friend's new beer festival. He was right; she'd seen William more recently. "Now now, no need to fight over me. I've got plenty of love to go around." With that, she released Billy and hugged William. "Besides, I just saw you this morning."

William gave her a warning glare. Billy wasn't supposed to know about the sailing lesson.

Billy pulled out a chair for Alex. "Oh? I didn't realize you'd seen each other already. Although I should have known, since William here didn't barrel over me to get to you."

Alex smiled sheepishly. "I wanted to make sure my shoes for Saturday met his standards. You know how he is." It wasn't a lie, not really. William had met her at her room before they went to the marina and she did show him what she'd be wearing.

Billy rolled his eyes, but then gave William an adoring look. "Yes, I certainly do know how he is."

William grinned, then his eyes focused outside and he tapped on the window again. Alex turned to see Cassidy and Reid as they approached the door, all grace and strength. As Alex got to know the archaeologists better, she understood why they were so fit. Their work involved a lot of physical activity.

William rushed around the table and ran directly to Reid, practically plowing him over. Billy shook his head and walked towards them more sedately. Cassidy shook his hand, then spread her arms in question. When he nodded, they embraced. William finally released Reid, who strode to Alex. She leaned in, sighing, then giving Cassidy a wink. Reid was gorgeous—tall, muscular without being bulky, with a surfer's bleached locks and piercing ice blue eyes. He smelled like sun-warmed leather. Despite his beauty and charm, he wasn't Alex's type. Good thing, since he was smitten with Cassidy.

And rightly so. Cassidy was one of the most powerful women—scratch that, people—Alex had ever met, both physically and mentally. She was a cougar in human form, and when she moved, it was with the barely contained agility of a feral beast.

Alex released Reid and he turned towards Billy. William wrapped his arm around his fiancé. "What'd I tell you? Gorgeous, aren't they?"

Billy smiled, a dimple appearing. "You must be Cassidy," he said, "and that means you, of course, are Reid. I've heard a lot about you."

"I bet you have," Cassidy said with a laugh. "Believe most of it."

Billy raised an eyebrow. Alex grinned. William could also raise just one at a time, unlike her. She always looked like she was in pain. "Are you sure?" Billy asked. "If you've met William, you know he's prone to hyperbole."

"Darling, I don't embellish; I merely emphasize."

"Well, you certainly emphasized a few things about them."

They all laughed, then took their seats. A server approached with menus, including a cocktail list. "I recommend the Oat Fashioned. It's our signature cocktail made with oat whisky."

"I second that recommendation," Alex agreed. "I mean, it's garnished with a Luxardo cherry–"

"And bacon," William interrupted. "Don't forget the bacon. Plus, when in Wisconsin, it's the law that you have to have at least one old fashioned."

"Just don't have so many you dance the polka on the bar," Billy warned. They all looked at him questioningly. "It's against the law."

"Seriously?" Alex asked.

Billy nodded. "Yep. There's still a statute on the books in Sheboygan prohibiting the dancing of the polka on bars."

William leaned in and kissed Billy on the cheek. "I love it when you talk law and order, my big burly po-liceman," he sighed.

Alex looked up at the young man, who was still waiting patiently to take their order. "I think we'll take five of those, please." After he left, she turned to Reid. "So, I heard you've found something exciting. Is it another shipwreck?"

William put his elbows on the table and rested his chin in his hands, blinking rapidly at the archaeologist. "Exciting? Do tell, do tell."

Reid laughed. Although they'd only met once before, he and Cassidy had quickly become enamored with William's antics. "It may be exciting, and it may be a shipwreck, but probably not the one you're thinking of."

Alex narrowed her eyes at Cassidy, thinking of their outing that afternoon. Cassidy subtly shook her head, which confirmed what Alex suspected. William caught the realization on her face. "What? What do you know? 'Fess up. It's my–"

"Our," Billy interjected.

"You're right, my love. It's *our* week, which means it's all about us, which means you have to tell us everything."

Reid laughed. "I don't think that's exactly how it works." He was saved by the arrival of their server, who distributed their cocktails and then listed the specials for that evening. Alex began, ordering the hangar steak with bacon hollandaise, served with roasted asparagus and boursin mashed potatoes. The rest called out with a chorus of "Same!" Before the young man left, William ordered a bottle of Cline Old Vines zinfandel for the table.

As they waited for their entrees, Cassidy and Reid shared stories of some of their most harrowing expeditions, including one to Guatemala that inspired their focus on indigenous cultures. They'd just launched into how they'd met Alex and William when the server dropped off a basket of truffle fries. "On the house," he explained, because their entrees were taking longer than expected. Alex looked around the room, realizing that it had filled while they'd been catching up with each other. She finished her scan, her eyes landing on the people lined up at the bar, and she froze.

There, sitting at the end, Ben lifted his rocks glass topped with bacon and a Luxardo cherry, and winked.

Chapter 4

Alex balled her fist. William noticed immediately. He spun around to see what she was staring at, then whipped his head back to her. "What is he doing here?"

"He *said* he's on assignment," she muttered through clenched teeth. "He *said* it's just a coincidence."

"You knew he was here?" Cassidy asked.

Alex nodded, her eyes still focused on her ex. "He approached me at the yacht club after our lunch today."

"Why didn't you say anything when we met later?" Cassidy asked.

Alex twinged, feeling a touch of sadness that she hadn't confided in her. She reached across the table to squeeze Cassidy's hand. "I didn't want to ruin our time together. And I didn't want to think about it."

"Fair enough."

Billy, who'd turned to face the bar at the same time William did, maintained his stony glare at Alex's ex. "Would you like me to say something?" he asked, keeping his focus on him. "I may not have jurisdiction, but I do have friends in the force here."

"And I'll back you up," Reid said, also glaring.

"No, absolutely not." The conviction in Alex's voice caused Billy to turn back and face her. She swept her gaze around the table, looking at each of her friends in turn. "You two are getting married this weekend. I will not have you doing anything but celebrating each other, got it?"

"You're kidding, right?" William said. "This is you we're talking about. You, Alex Paige. If anything happens to you because of that, that—"

"Neanderthal," Billy growled, using one of William's most oft-used insults.

"Yes, that Neanderthal, we would never forgive ourselves, and there's no way we can go on acting like everything's normal. I told you in Montana—he has taken his stalking to a dangerous level. I don't trust him. Please," he begged, gripping her hands, "please take this seriously. I know you think he's harmless, but c'mon. You've got to see this is outrageous behavior."

Alex sighed. She squeezed William's hands and extracted hers. "It is outrageous, and yes, frankly, I am concerned. But this is between Ben and me, and I'm going to put a stop to it right now."

With that, Alex stood. She put her napkin next to her plate, smoothed the wrinkles out of her blouse, and faced Ben. Since he was still staring at her, they made eye contact immediately. She turned away and walked towards the entrance of the restaurant, feeling her friends' eyes following her every move. Before the door had even closed, through the cacophony of the crowded restaurant she heard the legs of a barstool scraping against the floor.

Alex moved over to stand in front of the window so her friends could see her. She might be willing to confront Ben on her own, but she also knew they needed to know what was happening, and she needed the comfort of their concern. As she waited, she focused on the blinking marquee of the theater across the street and breathed deeply, her arms crossed over her chest. The door opened and the sound of conversation from inside the restaurant reached her. Alex flung her hair back, shaking her hands loose and inhaling through her nose, filling her body with determination. She turned to face Ben. He approached her, his stride slow and leisurely, a sly grin on his face.

"I knew you couldn't resist me," he said.

Alex put her hand out. "Stop. Right there."

Ben tilted his head. "So that's how we're going to play it, eh? Hard to get? You know as well as I do the game is over."

"This isn't a game, Ben, but you're right about one thing. It *is* over."

"See? I knew you'd see the light. This was all just temporary insanity. Understandable, really, with all those chemicals they pumped into you."

"Those chemicals saved my life. And they have and had nothing to do with us. Except that during that time I was able to see who you really were, and you keep showing me who you are." Alex spoke calmly, almost sadly. He really wouldn't get it.

"I'm someone who loves you, Alex. That's who I am."

Alex threw her head back and laughed. "Oh, Benjamin, you wouldn't know love if it came with turn-by-turn directions plotted into your GPS and a blinking neon sign shouting "LOVE HERE." The only person you care about is yourself and what you want. And you've got it into your sick little mind that you want me. I don't know why, and I don't care, but this is over."

As Alex spoke, anger slowly washed over Ben's face. He leaned closer, snarling. "Like you know anything about love. I did everything for you. Everything. I brought you flowers every week, but did that matter to you? No. But I was still there for you. Why do you think I went to Door County? To Montana? To here? These stupid stories mean nothing to me."

Alex leaned back, alarmed by his vehemence, but she refused to back down. "There it is. All those protests about 'it's not about you' were just that: feeble protests. You're a stalker, Ben." She considered him, looking him up and down as he'd done to her so many times. Where his had been to assess her physical attributes, to express his lust, she appraised the wholeness of him. "You have no empathy, no love, no kindness. I want nothing to do with you; I will *never* want anything to do with you. You're wasting your time. Goodbye, Ben. For the last time, goodbye."

Alex moved to walk around him, belatedly realizing she'd made a mistake. She shouldn't have let him come between her and the door. He grabbed her arm, pulling her in close. "That's where you're wrong. This isn't goodbye. It's never goodbye. You can't get away from me." He spoke into her ear and his breath, reeking of whiskey and venom, was so hot she felt like her skin was burning. She yanked her arm back, but he wouldn't release it, his fingers digging into her flesh. *Oh god*, she thought, too late. *William was right. He* is *dangerous*. The panic mounted. *Surely he wouldn't do anything here, not with all these people around.* She looked to the restaurant, noticing for the first time they had an audience. Several of the diners stood at the glass, watching their confrontation. William was already out of his chair and she caught his eyes, knowing he could see her fear. Ben tugged and she yanked her arm again.

"Let me go," she shouted. "Ben, let me go."

"You want me to let you go? Fine." He released her so abruptly she fell backwards, landing on the sidewalk. Ben laughed. "See what happens when I'm not holding you up? You are nothing without me."

This cauterized her fear. Alex sprang up, not even bothering to wipe the dirt from the concrete off her pants. This time, she leaned into him, pointing her finger in his face. "Don't you ever, ever touch me again. Do you hear me?"

"Or what?" he sneered. "You'll sic your little *boy*friend on me?"

Anger consumed Alex. For years she'd endured his condescension, his need to control her, never seeing it for what it was until chemotherapy and the vulnerability of fighting a life-threatening disease had stripped her raw. In William, in her parents, in her next door neighbor Emily and so many others, she'd seen what compassion, friendship, and love were supposed to be. Somehow, even though she'd become a shell of the strong person she'd been when she went on her first date with Ben, she could summon that woman from her past. Cancer may have weakened her body, but it strengthened her soul, and she rejected his treatment of her. After years of gradually wilting, she'd realized there was no way in hell she was supposed to be a frail little flower.

Alex heard the door open and knew her friends were filing out of the restaurant, lining up behind her. A flash of fear crossed Ben's eyes, confirming it, and she smiled with satisfaction. "No, Benjamin. I have no need to 'sic' anyone on you. You're not worth any of their attention, and you're certainly not worthy of mine." She walked up to him, getting within inches, finally brushing the dirt from her pants with a casual motion. She inhaled before putting her lips near his ear so she wouldn't breathe in any more of his scent than she had to. "I am and have always been stronger than you thought I was, and you have no control over me. You haven't for some time."

She pulled back, breathing in the fresh air. She could feel her friends' warmth. None of them said a word, and that made her love them even more. People like Benjamin Ainsworth couldn't imagine someone like Alex could stand up for herself. Her friends respected her enough to let her handle this on her own, while making their presence and solidarity known.

Ben seemed shocked. He was speechless, for once, but not for long. "This isn't over, Alex. I told you, you can't escape me. You belong to me."

Alex did the thing she knew would infuriate him the most. She laughed. Then she turned her back to him to face her friends. "Shall we go back inside? I have a feeling our dinner's going to be ready soon." She moved to join them when she felt his hand on her again. He grabbed her shoulder, swinging her around. *Enough!* a voice in her head screamed. Fear and adrenaline took over; her instinct for self-preservation kicked in. As she spun towards him, pulled by the force of his grip, she raised her hand, clenched it into a fist, and punched him in the face.

Chapter 5

"That was amazing! Here's a toast to Alex Paige, our KO champion," William cheered. Billy, Cassidy, and Reid lifted their glasses to join him, but Alex shook her head.

"I didn't knock him out," she protested.

"No, but you sure did knock him over," Cassidy said, her glass still in the air. "Now come on, lift that glass. If nothing else, we can celebrate you showed that SOB he can't mess with Alex Paige."

"Now that's something I will toast to." Alex smiled and lifted her glass to tap it against the other four. She took a sip of the velvety smooth red wine.

William narrowed his eyes at her. "Seems like somebody's been hiding something. When did you learn to throw a left hook like that?"

Alex grinned. "After Door County. I know it seemed like I brushed your concerns off, but I took them seriously. Especially when Ben showed up at my condo a few days after I got home."

"He did what?" William exclaimed, then looked out the window as if searching for Ben.

"It's fine. I didn't think it was a big deal, but your voice kept echoing in my head. Nagging me, really, so I began taking self-defense classes and found I like the physical activity."

William reached over and squeezed her bicep. "Nice. Well, good job."

Cassidy studied Alex. "Do you think he'll leave you alone now?"

"No. In fact, I probably just made things worse."

"*You* didn't make things worse," Reid said sternly. "This is all on him. You defended yourself and you have four witnesses to back you up, if necessary."

Billy cleared his throat. "Have you considered getting a restraining order?"

"I've thought about it, but do those even work?" she asked. As a police detective, Billy would have experience with these. Even though he was stationed in a sparsely populated location, it was also a tourist destination that drew millions each year. He'd probably seen his share of domestic abuse cases. Although Ben had never hit her, tonight he assaulted her, proving that things were escalating and she needed to put a stop to it.

"Honestly? Not all the time. But they do often act as a deterrent. Besides, you still know people at his paper. Can't imagine that would go over too well for a journalist covering corruption to have a restraining order against him."

Alex thought that was naïve, but she mulled it over. "I'll think about it. In the meantime, I believe we have some celebrating to do."

"I'll drink to that," William said. "Here's to wuv, twu wuv!" The friends laughed, raising their glasses again, the tension from Ben's confrontation diluted by William and Billy's happiness.

Alex took a bite of her steak, amazed at how tender it was and reveling in the richness of the bacon hollandaise sauce. "That is one of the best things I've ever put in my mouth." William inhaled as if to speak, and Alex pointed her fork at him. "Stop right there, mister." She grinned, then turned to Cassidy. "So, did you tell Reid where we went today?"

Cassidy nodded, chewing and swallowing before speaking. "I second that. That steak is—sublime. And yes, I sure did."

Reid leaned forward, his face animated with excitement. "We knew about it, of course. It's one reason we're here. Besides your wedding, of course," he stammered. "Of course, that's the real reason we're here."

William waved it off. "I have no illusions about any of you," he said. "Billy and I know you're here to celebrate, but all three of you are Type A and there's no way you're going somewhere without diving—ba dum bum—into your passions."

Billy raised his glass. "Spoken like a true Type A himself."

"Takes one to know one," Alex said, lifting hers in response. "If you're not looking for European shipwrecks, what are you hoping to find?" When Cassidy and Reid grinned at each other, Alex realized they already had. "Or have already found?"

A silent conversation passed between the archaeologists, and they must have decided it was fine to talk about it. "We did find something extraordinary," Cassidy said. "We've been researching trade among the early Americans."

"As in First Peoples, not United States Americans," Reid explained.

"Shells from Peru have been found in Hopewell Mounds sites in Ohio. Copper artifacts from upstate New York have shown up in Mississippian sites in the southeast. We knew it made sense the Great Lakes would be a frequently used path."

"Frequently?" William asked. "These were primitive cultures, weren't they? How frequent could they have been?"

Cassidy's eyes flared. "Primitive by whose definition? What we were taught about the original inhabitants was myth and propaganda, and we don't have enough wine to get into that."

"Let's just say we found proof that Lake Michigan was indeed a trade route, dating back at least a thousand years," Reid said.

Billy choked on his water. "A thousand years?"

Reid grinned. "Yep. And we found something today that'll prove it."

"What?" Alex asked. Cassidy and Reid eyed each other again. "You can't leave us hanging—you've got to tell us now."

Reid nodded and Cassidy spoke. "It's hard to tell because we couldn't get too close, but we believe we found a dugout canoe. From where it's settled, we're guessing it's from around 800 to 1000 CE."

Alex's eyes widened. "The same time period as those mounds."

"Yep. Exactly."

"So what's next?" William asked. "Will you bring it to the surface?"

Reid hedged. "Well, that may be an issue. It's buried right next to one of those historic shipwrecks."

"But that's not the biggest problem," Cassidy explained. "They're both about 450 feet underwater, which is why we have to use the ROV. Divers can't go deeper than a hundred and thirty."

"Plus," Reid said, "that shipwreck is pretty special. It's got the largest number of Nash automobiles in existence, so working around it is fraught with all sorts of complications."

"Wait, I've heard of that. The, what is it, the S.S. Senator, right?" Billy asked. William beamed with pride.

"Exactly," Reid confirmed. "It went down in 1929 with 265 of them, and they're still there."

Alex studied them, remembering their interaction at lunch. "I could tell earlier you'd encountered a problem. Was that it?"

Reid shook his head. "No, we always knew about the Senator. In fact, that's how we came across the canoe. After you so graciously invited us to your wedding," he said to William, "we began researching the area and found a video of the shipwreck. Cassidy noticed something that didn't seem to fit, and well, here we are."

"So, what was the issue?"

"Ever the reporter," Cassidy said, smiling with a slight shake of her head. "It's probably nothing."

"In other words, you're not going to tell me."

Cassidy winked. "You got it."

The server approached. After they declined dessert, William protesting that he had a tux to fit into, they paid their bill. As they stood to leave, they all focused on Alex.

"I don't think it's a good idea for you to stay by yourself tonight," William said.

"I'll be fine. You really think he'd come after me at the resort?"

"Yes," the four of them chorused.

"You punched him," Reid said.

"It was self-defense."

"We know that," Reid replied, "but you knocked him flat in front of not only us, but a whole restaurant full of people. I may have never met the man, but I know people like him, and he's not going to let that go."

"I can't hide from him my whole life."

"No, but you can take precautions," Billy said, his voice deep and filled with conviction. "You can obviously take care of yourself, but what if he comes after you with a gun? You need to be careful."

Alex bristled. She hated it when people told her what she needed to do, but she also knew Billy was right. During dinner she'd put the altercation with Ben out of her mind, as much as she could, but he'd truly scared her. He'd taken his psychological abuse to the physical level, and she didn't want to take the chance that he'd go even further than grabbing her. "Fine. What do you suggest?"

"Stay with us," Cassidy said. "We've got a guest berth."

"Just how big is your boat?" William asked.

"Big enough to make sure Alex is safe tonight." Cassidy took Alex's hands. "Please. I can loan you something to sleep in. If you won't stay for yourself, stay for us." Next to her, Reid nodded.

"Just a warning," Reid began.

"What, you snore like a chainsaw?" William asked. "I knew you couldn't be totally perfect."

Reid chuckled, then focused on Alex again. "Once you go boat, you'll always want to float."

The friends groaned. With that, Alex made her decision. "Fine. One night. Just tell me you have coffee."

"Of course," Cassidy answered. "It's even fresh from Guatemala."

"Now you're speaking my language. I may just sign on as a deckhand."

Alex skirted a puddle, its thawing surface reflecting the early moments of the sunrise as it crested the horizon. Her legs were a little wobbly from being on the boat all night, and she hadn't quite gotten her land-legs back yet. By the time they'd gotten to the catamaran the night before, the wind had picked up enough to concern Alex. Turned out, she had one of the best nights of sleep of her life, lulled like a baby in a bassinet.

She paused to set her cup down and get out her phone. She needed to capture the moment, especially the way the ice at the edges of the puddle sparkled. Her berth in the catamaran had been nice and warm, but watching the day awaken was her ritual. When the temperature had gotten below freezing before they'd gone to bed, Cassidy had loaned her a couple of sweatshirts and some fleece-lined pants. With that and a hot beverage, Alex was cozy enough to greet the day.

She framed the view, the edge of the lake lined with rich orange that bled into a deep blue. At the end of the breakwater, a squat red lighthouse broke the even plane. A seagull flew past at the exact moment she took her picture, and she grinned. She picked up her coffee again, inhaling the aroma. It was truly one of the best cups of coffee she'd ever had.

After a night on the catamaran with Cassidy and Reid, she understood the allure of living aboard. Could she do it, though? Could she be truly nomadic like the couple, living half the year on a luxury yacht and the other half traveling in an RV? Probably not; she enjoyed coming home to her cat and her condo after every trip. But it would be nice every once in a while.

Despite her best efforts, the archaeologists refused to tell her what had them so concerned the day before. They'd capped off the evening with a glass of port, 'because what else would we drink on a boat?' Reid had quipped. While they hadn't stayed up too late, there'd been enough time to catch up on the last several months since they'd first met in Gulf Shores. Alex asked about LuEllen, Cassidy's much older sister and the reason they'd met in the first place. Cassidy just shook her head, saying LuEllen was LuEllen and what else did you really need to know?

Alex smiled, thinking of the boisterous chef and her Shrimp Shack, which was now expanding, as planned, around the Gulf of Mexico. She'd have to get back down to see her again soon. Her memories and thoughts of her friend distracted her as she continued walking towards the lighthouse, taking her phone out every few moments to shoot more photos. Even though she'd been to Sheboygan before, the view always surprised her. It was hard to believe the vast expanse was a freshwater lake and she hadn't been instantly transported to the coast.

It was a windy morning. Waves hit the breakwater, spraying water over the rocks and the flat surface that led to the lighthouse. Fortunately, there were still enough dry patches that she could walk without slipping and it looked like the frozen puddles had melted, nor was it windy enough for her to be concerned she'd be blown into the water. She did, however, have to watch where she stepped. Her tailbone was still sore from her fall the night before. Alex shivered, not from the cool air, but from the memory of Ben's anger, from his assault. The word felt like an exaggeration, but she knew it wasn't. He *had* physically assaulted her. She smiled grimly as she thought of her punch, and how good it felt when her fist connected solidly with his jaw. Not that she felt good about using violence, but that she had stood up for herself. Ben had become increasingly invasive, and with last night's behavior, she had felt genuine fear. At least she'd taken precautions and learned how to defend herself, but Billy was right: that wouldn't do much good if he had a gun.

Alex shook her head, trying to clear those disturbing thoughts. It was an absolutely beautiful morning; she had a delicious cup of coffee, a stunning sunrise, and the oversized sweatshirts felt soft and cozy against her skin. Her best friend was getting married in three days, her other best friend would be there in two, and friends she saw infrequently would all be gathering to celebrate William and Billy. Except for Ben, all was right with her world.

She took another sip of her coffee, letting the liquid warm her from within. More seagulls flew past as the morning awakened. *This is the perfect way to start the day*, she thought. She decided she should probably head back to the catamaran. Her friends had still been asleep when she left and she didn't want them to wake up and be worried, even though they knew this was her plan. Alex took one last deep breath, then turned around to face the shore. The piled boulders that formed the breakwater were awash in yellows and oranges, broken by shadows. She squatted to get a better perspective. As she moved her phone to line up the proper frame, she noticed an anomaly among the rocks. It was smooth, in contrast to the rough contours. Something was lodged between two boulders. *What is that*, she wondered. It looked like the waves had washed up a blanket, and she wondered if it had blown off someone's boat.

She zoomed in. No. Oh no. That was definitely not a blanket. She stood, then slowly picked her way closer. Another wave crashed against the rocks, shifting whatever it was, pushing it even further onto the breakwater, wedging it between the boulders. Alex gasped. No no no. It can't be. No!

As she moved closer, it took shape, and she wondered how she could have thought it was a blanket, or anything but what–or who–it really was.

Chapter 6

"E arth to Alex."

She blinked, then tore her eyes away from the view outside the window. She'd been staring in the direction of the lighthouse, but hadn't seen it. Instead, the image of a man's body being buffeted by the waves filled her vision. Alex had hesitated, just a moment, before moving closer, close enough to grab his arms and pull him completely out of the water. She briefly wondered if she'd get in trouble for disturbing the body, but decided it would be even worse if he was swept into the lake. She gently rolled him over, then collapsed next to him, staring at his face.

It was Ben.

Scratches marred his skin. She noticed pebbles stuck in his hair and carefully removed them. Alex had no idea how long she'd sat there before she remembered she needed to call 911. She'd call William first—NO, she reprimanded herself. She couldn't call him. She *wouldn't* call him. Instead, she'd called the police, then called Cassidy. By the time the officers and EMTs had arrived, Cassidy and Reid had brought two warm blankets, one for her and the other to cover Ben.

"Hello? Somebody's in la-la land. Are you still thinking about Ben?" William asked gently.

"What? No. I mean yes. I mean, I don't know."

William walked to her and wrapped his arms around her. "It's okay to be shaken. Last night was awful. Did those two take good care of you?"

Alex tried to gather herself. She hadn't told him yet about what had happened that morning. She wiped her eyes, angry that tears had started to form. They had all gathered in William and Billy's suite to be fitted for their tuxes and gowns. All except Billy, who went to the marina to meet Juke and Evie, friends of theirs from Door County, where Billy lived and was a detective. Billy had asked Juke to be his best man, and he and William had invited Evie. It took a moment for Alex to process what William had asked her. "You mean Cassidy and Reid? They were immaculate hosts, of course."

William narrowed his eyes at her. "And how was that legendary coffee?"

"Coffee?" Alex pictured the mug she'd set down on the concrete next to Ben's head. When she'd remembered to pick it up again, the liquid was ice cold. "Oh yes, the coffee. It was fine."

"That's it, Alex Paige. You will tell me right here and right now what's going on."

"Nothing's going on," she said, knowing he wouldn't buy it.

"Not buying that for a second. If there's one thing I know about you, it's how much you love your coffee. So give it up. What's wrong?"

Alex shifted her eyes to glance at Cassidy, who gave her a small, encouraging smile. Still, she hesitated.

"Is it Ben? Did he find you?"

Alex immediately broke into tears. William wrapped his arms around her and she sobbed. She hadn't cried that morning. Not a single drop. She'd admonished herself. Was she so immune, was she so angry, was she so bereft of feelings for Ben that she couldn't summon a single display of sorrow?

That answered that.

William guided her to one of the sofas and helped her sit down. He held her until she'd cried it all out, then pulled a handful of tissues from the box Cassidy had placed on the coffee table. After she'd pulled herself together, she wiped the mascara from under her eyes. "I should have known I couldn't keep it from you."

His face filled with anger and she felt his shoulders stiffen. "What did he do? I'll kill the SOB if he so much as touched you again."

"No need," Alex said.

Realization hit him. "Is he... what happened?" William sought out Cassidy and Reid. "Somebody tell me. What happened to Ben? Did he come after her again? Did he find your boat?" He stood up. "What happened?"

Reid crossed the room and put his hands on William's shoulders. "First of all, no, he didn't find us. Alex went for a walk to the lighthouse this morning."

"To see the sunrise."

Alex reached up and took William's hand. "You know me so well." He looked down at her, squeezing her fingers gently.

"And?"

"Ben's body was on the breakwater," Reid explained.

William stared at him. He looked dumbfounded. "When she was there? He just happened to be where she was out walking? That's taking stalking to a whole new level." His attempt at levity fell flat. "Sorry. I don't know how to handle this."

"That's why I didn't want to tell you," Alex said. "This is the last thing you need to be worried about."

"This is you, Alex, and don't you dare try to protect me when you're going through something like this." William looked at her sternly, but she knew it was only because he truly cared for her. "Now, details. You were walking and his body just washed up?"

Alex shook her head. "No. I guess it may have. I don't know how long he was there. I didn't see him when I walked toward the lighthouse, but he was wedged between two boulders," her voice hitched, "and the one closer to shore was bigger, so he would have been hidden."

William nodded, picturing the scene. "I assume you called the police?"

"That's why we were late," Cassidy said. "You know how long those things take."

"Sadly, I do." William sat back down next to Alex. "I'll get straight to the point. You found him, and you're his ex. Are you a suspect?"

"They didn't say I was."

"They did say to make sure you're available in case they had more questions," Reid said.

Alex sighed, slumping her shoulders. "Yes, they did say that."

"Of all the places for him to show up, why did you have to be the one to find him? I've heard of bad pennies, but this is ridiculous," William grunted.

"That is a good question, though. What was he doing there?" Cassidy asked.

"I don't know. He said he was working on some big story, and since I saw him yesterday at the yacht club, maybe it had something to do with the marina, or somebody at the marina."

"He's always working on some big story when he just happens to be where you are," William said.

"Happened to be," Alex corrected. "But you're right. It seems far too coincidental."

"Makes me wonder if he put a tracker on your Outback."

Cassidy and Reid stared at William, then looked at each other. Without a word they left the room. William and Alex followed, Alex quickly taking the lead so she could take them to her car. "Do you really think?" she asked. "It would explain a lot."

"Not his appearance in Montana. You flew there," William said.

"Except I was on the list of speakers. It was pretty obvious where I'd be."

"True. Okay. What do we need to do?" William asked. In answer, Reid bent over and ran his hands under the back bumper.

"Well, look who I found!" They all looked up to see Billy approaching with a handsome, rugged man and a petite redheaded woman. Billy stopped as he noticed what Reid was doing. "Is there a problem with Alex's car?"

"Maybe," William said, walking over and taking his fiancé's hand. "Ben's dead," he said without preamble. "Alex found him this morning."

Billy's head snapped to face Alex, his demeanor abruptly changing. She recognized it as his cop-mode. "What happened?"

She gave him a brief description, which he interrupted with questions, including the exact time she found Ben, which she had because she'd taken a picture right before encountering his body. Billy also asked about the police that had arrived on the scene. He nodded. "I know Stephens. She's good. Tough, but good."

"That's the feeling I got from her."

"She seemed a bit harsh to me," Cassidy said.

Alex gave her a small smile. "She's just doing her job. She doesn't know me, and since I found the body, well. Plus, she wasn't nearly as bad as that officer, what was his name? Rourke? Now he was a real jerk."

"Does Stephens know Ben was your ex, and that he'd been stalking you?" Billy asked. Alex half expected him to pull out a pen and a notebook.

"No. Sort of. She knows we saw him last night."

"Did you tell her about the argument, and that he assaulted you?"

"And that I punched him? No, I knew better than that," Alex said.

Billy crossed his arms, drumming his fingers on his biceps. "She'll find out anyway. Probably wouldn't be a bad thing to let her know before she finds out from someone else."

Alex sagged. She knew he was right, but she also knew it would put her in the crosshairs. She definitely had motive; the man had been following her across the country for the last year and a half, and he'd gotten downright threatening the night before.

The two friends who'd arrived with Billy had been standing awkwardly behind him, but when Alex's posture shifted to obvious distress, the redhead walked to her, then held her tightly. Alex pulled back, wiping a few tears from her cheeks. "Thanks, Evie. Sorry you had to walk in on something like this."

Evie shook her head. "There's nothing to apologize for."

The rugged man joined them, and when he hugged Alex, she felt like she could stay there all day. She finally pulled back. "Hey, Juke."

"Hey."

Alex had to smile. He'd always been a man of few words. She looked questioningly at Evie. The two had been high school and college sweethearts, but as often happens, had split up. When Alex had met them, Evie's fiancé had been murdered and she and Juke had both been suspects. After the real murderer was found, there'd seemed to be a possibility the two would get back together, but as far as Alex knew, it hadn't happened yet. She wondered if their arrival together was a good sign. She couldn't think of two people more suited for each other, despite, or maybe because of, their differences.

The petite woman shook her head, telling Alex that no, they weren't an item. Yet. Alex still held out hope the two would get together, and she knew Billy did, too. Juke was Billy's best man, and if anyone knew how he felt about the tiny redhead, it was William's fiancé.

"OK," Billy said, back to business, "I'm assuming you're looking for a tracker?"

A moment of astonishment crossed Reid's face, and William grinned. "He's really, really good at his job."

"I guess so," Reid said. "Yes. We're wondering how he always knew where Alex would be, even though she'd blocked him on social media."

"If I had my cruiser with me, I'd have the equipment to make finding this easier."

"Should we ask Detective Stephens?"

"Not yet," Billy answered immediately. "Knowing that Ben was stalking Alex would immediately put her at the top of the suspect list, especially after last night's altercation. At least, that's what I'd do."

"Good thing you're on our side," Reid said.

Billy turned his attention to Reid. "I'm on the side of catching whoever did this, and I know Alex didn't."

Alex settled with relief. Until that moment, she hadn't realized she'd been concerned that Billy would doubt her. She should have known better; she'd gotten to know him pretty well in the last year and a half. She also knew William was a great judge of character, and he'd never commit to someone who wouldn't give friends the benefit of the doubt. He'd still be thorough, but he'd also trust his own instincts.

Billy continued. "Do you know what you're looking for?"

Reid nodded. "We've had our share of stalkers over the years." When Billy raised an eyebrow, he explained. "We've had a few digs that have upset some people."

"We find things that change the standard narrative of what this hemisphere was like before the Europeans arrived. Tends to ruffle some feathers," Cassidy said.

"To put it mildly. So yes, I know what to look for."

Billy nodded. "Hold on just a sec. I have gloves in my car." He jogged over to a black SUV.

"You didn't drive Bessie down?" Alex asked William.

"Nah. No need for a campervan when we're staying here. Plus, his car gets better gas mileage."

When Billy returned, he handed a pair of blue gloves to Reid. "I'll take the front. You take the rear."

"Got another pair?" Cassidy asked. "I can take the sides." She snapped hers on and disappeared behind the passenger side.

Billy walked to the front of Alex's car, stopping to open the door so he could pop the hood. He checked his watch, then turned to Alex. "This could take some time. Why don't you go back to the room? They should be delivering lunch pretty soon."

Alex hesitated as her three friends got to work, then shook herself off. "You heard the man," she said, with false bonhomie. "Let's let them do their thing."

"I hope they didn't forget the bubbly, because I could certainly use a drink," William said.

"You and me both."

They walked towards the entrance when Alex stopped and spoke to Evie and Juke. "Oh. I forgot to introduce you to Cassidy and Reid."

Evie threaded her arm through Alex's, turning to look back at the three people who were all laying on their backs. "We can meet them later. C'mon. Let's get you something to eat. I have a feeling you haven't had a thing all day."

Alex nodded almost absently. Evie's words brought her back to the breakwater. She shuddered, then followed William down the hall toward the elevators, passing her room along the way. *If nothing else*, she thought, *I can stay in my room now.*

Chapter 7

Juke answered the knock on the door and a pair of servers wheeled in carts laden with food. They distributed trays of fruit, hummus and vegetables, caprese skewers, mini-sandwiches, and a bowl filled with spinach salad. They also set up a mimosa bar and a tub filled with varieties of sparkling water.

"Fancy," Juke said.

William grinned. "You know how I roll."

"I'm learning. I have to say, the change in Billy since you two met has been remarkable."

"Oh? I never meant to change him. I love him just the way he is."

Juke shook his head. "It's a good thing. You haven't changed who he is, just how comfortable he is with being who he is, if that makes sense."

William thought about it. "Maybe."

"He's much more relaxed," Evie explained. "More lighthearted."

"But still oh-so-serious about his job."

"I've noticed," Alex said. "Did you see how quickly he changed gears down there? It's like someone flipped a switch."

William grinned. "He does get very serious when he's in Mr. Police mode. I love it."

"What I'm trying to say," Juke fumbled, "is that you're really good for him."

"Aww!" William ran over and tackled Juke in a big hug. Although the other man was a couple of inches taller, William himself was well-built and he practically knocked him over. "And here I thought you didn't approve."

Juke extracted himself. "You're one-of-a-kind, I'll give you that. And I know you'll take good care of each other."

"You better believe it," William wiggled his eyebrows, and they all laughed. The door opened and Billy entered. "Speak of the devil. Handsome devil, I mean." William stopped when he saw the expression on Billy's face.

"I'm sorry," Billy paused, "We found a tracker."

Alex exhaled. That answered how Ben had always been able to find her. She still wondered why, except for once, he never bothered her at her condo, or even when she was in Chicago, since that's where they both lived. "At least now I know." She searched Billy's hands, but they were empty. "Where is it? You didn't leave it on there, did you?" Her voice rose in panic.

Billy spoke calmly. "We need to call Detective Stephens and have her team take care of it."

Alex had started shaking her head before he'd finished. "No. No. Absolutely not. I'm not leaving that thing on my car for one more second." She pushed past Billy and left the room, practically running to the stairs because she couldn't stand to wait for the elevator. She heard footsteps behind her.

"Alex, wait," Billy called.

She ignored him and raced down the steps, then pushed the door and ran to her car. Once she got there, she realized she didn't know where the tracker was. She turned to see Billy, followed closely by Cassidy, Reid, and William. "Where is it? Show me. Where is it?"

Billy slowed down as he neared her. "Hold on, Alex. It's going to be allright."

"No it isn't!" she screamed, fighting back tears. "He'd been tracking me, like I'm some animal. I don't want it on my car for one more second. Where is it?"

Billy hesitated. The other three waited. "Fine. I get it. I understand, okay? Let me get another pair of gloves and an evidence bag. But you have to promise me you'll take it to Detective Stephens."

She nodded, willing herself to calm down. She knew he was right, and as a police officer himself, he had to do what he could to preserve any evidence, but she didn't have to be happy about it. She started to get into the car.

"Alex, you haven't eaten all day. Why don't you come upstairs first and then take it in after you've had a bite? William asked.

She sagged. "I just want to get rid of it."

William walked to her and took her hands. "I know, but you know what it's like at police stations. You could be waiting for hours. Please. For me?"

Alex acquiesced, then looked at Billy. "I'll call after I eat to tell her I'm coming, unless you think I absolutely have to go right now."

Billy gave Alex a sad smile. "He's right. You might be there for awhile. Better to see her without being hungry. Besides, if I disagree, I'll never hear the end of it from this one," he said, jabbing his thumb in William's direction.

"You got that right. You may be a cop, but this is Alex."

"Understood." Billy went to his car to get the items, then returned and got on his back under the rear bumper. Alex could see him pull out his phone and figured he was going to take a picture. When he stood back up, he put the device in the plastic bag. He handed it and an extra pair of gloves to Alex. "Leave it in the bag, but if it rips or anything–which it shouldn't–put these on before touching it."

Alex nodded. She was tempted to hand the bag back to him, but instead forced herself to look at it. Ben really had gone too far. If he hadn't been killed, how much further would he have taken his obsession? She shivered. While she wasn't glad he was dead, she'd be lying to herself if she didn't admit that she was relieved that she didn't have to worry about him stalking her any more.

The friends headed back upstairs to the suite. Alex went straight to the sideboard where the servers had set up the mimosa bar and poured herself a glass of champagne, ignoring the orange, cranberry, and pomegranate juices. She carried her glass to the windows and looked out again at the lighthouse and the break-water leading up to it. She felt someone stand next to her and glanced down to see Evie. The petite woman's experience finding her ex's body had been eerily similar to Alex's, although Alex had broken up with Ben two years ago and not the night before, like Evie had. The redhead had also gotten in a very public fight, like Alex, which made finding his body the next morning even worse.

"It seems we have another thing in common," Evie said.

"I would have been fine keeping it as fellow breast cancer survivors."

"You and me both." Evie looked up at her. "I'm so sorry. I know how conflicted you're feeling right now."

Alex nodded. "Conflicted is right. I wanted him to leave me alone, but I didn't want this to happen to him. I didn't want him to die." She took a drink, then set her glass down. She wanted to have a clear head when she called Detective Stephens. "So, you know I have to ask..." she started, wanting a distraction.

"About Juke?" Evie turned and found him across the room, standing at the sideboard and filling a plate. "We're just friends."

"Is he okay with that? Are you?"

Evie resumed looking out the window and nodded. "Yes. I needed time alone after Nick. Now I just want time alone. I've found I like it."

Alex agreed. "It's nice not having to answer to anybody, isn't it?"

"Yes, but..."

"Yeah," Alex said wistfully. "It would also be nice to have someone to share everything with. I mean, I do have that, with Emily and William."

"But it's not the same."

"No, it isn't. I'm happy, though, being single."

"Me, too. Should we get something to eat?"

Alex nodded. She took one last long look at the lake, then turned to join her friends.

Alex paced in the lobby of the police station, wondering how many times, in how many police stations, she'd walked back and forth, back and forth, waiting to be questioned, waiting for answers, waiting. The receptionist picked up a ringing phone, then spoke to her. "Detective Stephens is ready for you." He gave Alex directions and she walked through the buzzing door. Officer Rourke, the same officer who'd been so rude to her that morning, waited for her. Cassidy, Reid, and Evie tried to follow. "Only Ms. Paige, please," Rourke said, his tone clipped.

Juke and the happy couple had remained at the resort. Although they'd insisted on joining her, Alex was even more insistent that they stay in the suite and do what they needed to do. The tailor would be fitting them that afternoon, and there was no way Alex would allow them to skip it. "I'll have these three with me," she said. "If you three come, too, they'll definitely think I've got something to hide. What innocent person needs an entire entourage? Even three is too much."

"Tough. We're going with you, and that's that," William said.

"Billy, please talk some sense into him. Scratch that." She stood in front of William and gave him her sternest look. "You are going to stay here. You are going to get fitted for your tux. You are getting married in three days, and I know you've planned everything with precision."

"At least Billy could go. He knows Detective Stephens."

"And then it'll look even more like I've got something to hide. No." Alex softened. "Please. Knowing that you're getting all dolled up to marry the love of your life will help me focus on something good and happy. I *need* you to stay here. Please?"

William relented. "Fine. But you better call me as soon as you're out. And if she doesn't," he said, facing Cassidy, Reid, and Evie, "one or, better yet, all three of you better call me."

Chapter 8

Alex walked down the hall, Officer Rourke behind her. It was so quiet the only sounds were the thud of his shoes hitting the linoleum and a muted conversation in the distance. The volume increased as they neared a closed door. The officer knocked. "Come in," the voice said. The woman at the desk ended her call and looked up as Alex entered. "Have a seat. Thanks, Kyle. I'll buzz if I need anything."

Alex caught Officer Rourke's frown before he closed the door, a little aggressively, she thought. She settled into her chair, feeling Detective Stephens' eyes on her. She was surprised they were meeting in her office and not in an interrogation room, hoping that was a good sign. She knew from her days as an investigative reporter and her recent experiences with murder investigations she was the most likely suspect. It probably wasn't wise for her to meet with the detective without an attorney present, but it was too late for that now. She reminded herself to be very careful about what she said.

"Thanks for meeting me here, Ms. Paige. I've got an appointment in," she consulted the clock on the wall, "thirty minutes, and it's non-negotiable. One of those political la-ti-das that are a necessary evil nowadays." She stood up and walked to a wet bar embedded between floor-to-ceiling bookcases. "Would you like some tea? I was just brewing some for myself."

"Sure," Alex started, her voice catching. She cleared her throat. "I'd appreciate it."

The detective nodded and filled two mugs. "Cream? Sugar? It's a rooibos." When Alex declined, the detective brought the cups over. Instead of sitting behind her desk, she sat in the wingback chair next to Alex, slightly angled towards her.

"Now," the detective began, "you said you had something important to show me? Something related to Mr. Ainsworth?"

Alex nodded. She blew on the surface of her tea and took a sip, stalling briefly to try to gather her nerves. Although she knew she'd done nothing wrong, it was still hard to stay calm when she knew the woman next to her was tasked with finding a killer. "Yes, Detective Stephens."

"Please, call me Ophelia."

"Okay. Yes. Well, Ophelia, I told you this morning about my previous relationship with Ben," Alex began. When the detective nodded, she continued. "He didn't think it was over."

"What do you mean by that?"

"Let's just say Ben could be rather persistent. It's what makes—made—him a good reporter." Alex was surprised Ophelia wasn't taking notes and she wondered if she was being record-ed. No, can't be, she thought. That wouldn't be legal, and Billy wouldn't approve of the detective if she was the type to do some-thing like that. Alex cleared her throat. "I ended things about two years ago, but he kept showing up."

"Showing up? Where? At your home?" Ophelia reached across her desk to pluck a file sitting on top of a blotter. She opened it and flipped a few pages. "You live in Chicago, right? Lincoln Park, to be exact?"

Alex nodded. "Yes. And no, he wouldn't show up there. Only once, but that was over a year ago. He showed up in Door County last summer, and a few months ago he was in Montana when I was there."

"You said you're a travel writer. And Mr. Ainsworth was a reporter. Was it possible he was on assignment?"

"Oh, he was definitely on assignment. He'd conveniently be assigned to stories at the same time I'd be at a location."

Ophelia raised an eyebrow. "But you said he only showed up at your condo once. That seems a little, forgive me for saying—"

"Paranoid? I thought so, too. William kept warning me that Ben was stalking me, but I thought it was ridiculous. I didn't really believe it, not until last night, and it was confirmed this morning." Alex paused. That didn't come out right. She was definitely painting herself into a corner. "We, um, we had a confrontation last night."

"Oh?"

Alex sighed. This was not going how she'd intended. She really should have called a lawyer. Ethan was supposed to arrive that afternoon and she wondered if he was in town yet, although she didn't know if he could practice in Wisconsin. Even if he couldn't, his presence would have helped her keep her head about her. Alex took another sip of her tea and set the cup back on the desk, being careful to put it on a coaster instead of the burnished wood surface.

"I was at dinner with my friends and Ben was there. I knew then that he really was following me and he wouldn't stop unless I told him, with no question, that we were through, even though

I'd done that several times. We went outside and, well, he told me I was 'his,' and, and..." Alex's heart raced. The fear and the anger from the night before coursed through her. She still couldn't believe what he'd said, what he'd done. She closed her eyes and took deep breaths to calm herself, opening them only when she felt she could continue. Ophelia remained quiet, but Alex knew the detective was studying her and cataloging every reaction. "And I hit him."

Ophelia's eyes widened, almost imperceptibly, but enough for Alex to know the detective hadn't expected her to say that. It also told Alex that she already knew about the altercation. "He grabbed me." She rubbed her arm where he'd dug in, wincing as she brushed the tender spot. She pulled up her sleeve to display the bruises, five of them, where his fingers had squeezed.

"Ouch."

"He yanked me towards him, and I hit him. It was pure reflex. I, uh, I've been taking self-defense courses."

Ophelia nodded, and Alex thought she detected a hint of approval. "And then what happened?"

"My friends and I went back inside for dinner and I didn't see him again. They convinced me I shouldn't stay in my hotel room, and Cassidy and Reid—you met them—invited me to stay on their boat." That morning she'd told the detective about everything but the confrontation with Ben, and was sure Ophelia had confirmed it with her friends, but she felt she needed to repeat it.

"When you called, you said you had something to show me."

Alex reached into her purse and pulled out the evidence bag containing the tracker Billy had found on her car. "One of my friends suggested Ben may have been tracking me. They were right."

Ophelia accepted the bag. She stood up, walked around her desk, and picked up her phone. "Can you send Officer Rourke in, please? And tell him to bring an evidence bag." She put the handset back in its cradle, then sat in the chair behind her desk. Alex wondered if the friendly conversation they'd been having was now over and the interrogation would begin. The detective studied her thoughtfully before speaking. "Thank you for bringing this in. Which one of your friends found it?"

"Billy. Billy Pierce. He's a detective in Door County. I believe you know him?"

She nodded. "Yes, I do. He's good."

"That's what he said about you."

Ophelia smiled. "Is that why you're here without an attorney?"

"It's one reason. I just want to find out who did this. I know I'm probably a suspect," Alex said. Ophelia stayed silent, and this time her features didn't betray her. "And I will be contacting an attorney, just in case, but I wanted to get this to you right away, and I didn't want it to seem like I was hiding something. That would only make things worse."

"You're right about that." She leaned forward to get her cup from the other end of her desk, then leaned back in her chair again. "Who do you think did it? Who do you think killed Ben?"

Alex tilted her head slightly in surprise. It was the first time the detective had used his first name. Plus, the police usually didn't ask her who she suspected. They usually told her to stay out of it. "Honestly?"

"That would be best."

"I mean, of course I'll be honest," Alex said, with a touch of exasperation. At herself, not Ophelia. "I don't know. But, Ben's an investigative reporter. He's always digging into stories of corruption. Even the last time I saw him, in Montana, he was working on a story about a truly dangerous man. That's where I'd start—not that you're asking my opinion."

"I did, actually. That's helpful."

Alex could see why Billy liked her, and she decided to do something she normally wouldn't. "If you'd like, I can reach out to my contacts at his paper. I used to work there. It was years ago, but I still have some friends. I can try to find out what he was working on."

Ophelia hesitated. "I should say no. This is something we can do. But I have a feeling you're going to do it anyway, and even if I tell you not to, it won't do any good."

Alex smiled sheepishly. "You'd be correct. I was also an investigative reporter. Answering questions is what I do."

"Why did you stop?"

"It got to be too hard, too dark. I couldn't handle seeing all that wanton disregard for other people." She thought about her last case for the paper and shuddered. "Ben seemed to thrive on it, though. He always told me I was wasting myself by writing fru-fru travel pieces. I told him that people need joy, too."

"Yes, indeed they do. What is taking Kyle so long?" Ophelia muttered. She picked up the phone again, then set it down when there was a knock on her door. The officer entered and she frowned at him.

"Sorry." Although he said the word, it certainly didn't sound like he was, and he didn't explain what had taken him so long.

Ophelia frowned. She extended her hand for the evidence bag, filling out the case number and other details before depositing the tracker inside and handing it back to the officer. He signed it, then left the room. She took a card from a stand next to the phone and passed it to Alex. "I know you're in town for your friend's wedding."

"It's Billy, by the way," Alex interrupted. "Billy's getting married to William Blake, who's one of my best friends."

"Wait, Billy is marrying someone named William?" When Alex confirmed, she laughed. "Oh, I'll have to give him some grief about that."

Alex grinned. "You wouldn't be the first, or the last."

"I bet. Anyway, I don't think you have any plans to leave, but you know you need to stick around, at least until we have a more viable suspect. Because you're correct; at this time, you have motive and, since you were at the marina, opportunity."

"I know."

"But I'd also be really surprised to find out you were capable of murder. So here's what I want you to do. I want you to call your contacts at the paper and then get in touch with me after you find out what Mr. Ainsworth was working on."

"Will you be calling them, too?"

"Now, you know I can't divulge that, especially since I just told you you're my primary suspect." Ophelia stood up. Alex set her nearly full cup of tea, which was now cold, back on the coaster. The detective walked her towards the door. "I'll walk you out."

They reached the lobby. Cassidy, Reid, and Evie sprang up from their seats. Alex gave them a reassuring smile.

"Don't go too far, and remember to call me with what you find out. Are you going to be staying with these two?" she asked, indicating the tall couple.

Alex shook her head. "No. No need anymore," she said sadly. "I'm at the Blue Harbor." She looked at the detective's card and put it into her purse. "I'd ask you to keep me updated."

"But you know I can't do that. Tell Billy I said hi, and to give me a call, would you?"

Alex nodded, then left the station, her friends following closely behind. As soon as the door shut behind them, they started asking questions. Alex answered what she could, including that she was a suspect.

"That's ridiculous," Evie huffed. "Anyone can tell you're not a killer."

"I don't know; you should have seen her punch Ben last night," Reid teased.

"She did what?" Evie stopped in her tracks, then faced Alex. "You punched Ben? Now this I've gotta hear."

The three climbed into Cassidy and Reid's car, with Cassidy in the driver's seat. As they drove back to the hotel, they filled Evie in on what happened the night before.

Chapter 9

Alex gently closed the door to the suite and typed out a text as she walked back to her room. She would have contacted Tad, her friend at the Chicago Standard, when she got back from the station, but she knew the tailor was waiting for her in William and Billy's suite. As William's 'best person,' as he called it, she also needed to be fitted. Instead of a gown, Alex had elected to wear a suit as well. She smiled as she thought of her reflection in the perfectly tailored bespoke tuxedo. It wasn't traditional, but William wasn't the traditional type, nor would their marriage be. Billy would continue working as a detective and William would continue his life on the road writing about outdoor destinations, although he'd be slightly less nomadic. She'd asked him in the weeks leading up to the wedding how he felt about having a permanent home, considering he hadn't had one in years. "Good," he'd said. "Really, really good. I didn't think I had a single nesting bone in my body, but apparently, I like being in one place. Occasionally."

Alex had grinned. "Probably has something to do with who's in that one place."

"You got that right."

Alex finished her text, hoping she'd hear back from Tad soon. They kept in touch infrequently, but it was one of those relationships that didn't need constant nurturing. Most of her friendships were like that, which was a good thing since so many of her friends were scattered across the country, and even the world.

Her phone vibrated just as she reached the door to her room.

Now's good.

She dialed, and Tad picked up before the first ring had completed. "Hey there," he said, "how're you holding up?"

Alex stared at the phone, then shook her head with a smile. "I should have guessed you'd already heard about Ben."

"I work in a newsroom, after all. You didn't mention him in your text, but I figured that's why you wanted to talk."

"Yeah, I didn't think it would be very nice for you to learn about it in a text if you didn't know."

"Wouldn't have bothered me. You know how I feel, or I guess I should say felt, about the man."

"True, but you're also not heartless."

"Oh, I have my moments. Anyway, I'm assuming you want to know what he was working on?"

Alex laughed. "I'd forgotten how good you are."

"Just means we're overdue for dinner so you can be reminded. Again. I swear, every time we see each other my kids have grown several more inches." He paused, and Alex heard the tapping of his keyboard. "I'm shooting a quick email to his editor. You know his stories are always hush-hush, but Max owes me a favor."

"Thanks."

"So? How are you?"

"I'm fine. I think. It's hard to believe, you know?"

"I have to ask: are you a suspect?"

Alex sighed. She was going to start leading with that whenever she talked about Ben. *Guess what, my ex is dead, I found the body, and I'm the prime suspect.* "Of course. I found him."

"Oh, sweetie, I'm so sorry. The guy was a rotten jerk, but even so, I know at one point you thought he had some redeeming qualities." Tad cleared his throat. "Sorry, again, that was insensitive."

"It's fine. Really. But that's why I need to know what he was working on. If I can find out who had motive, or who else had motive, I should say, it'll get me off the hook."

"Ah—got a response already." Tad paused to read the email. "Have you heard of the Wisconsin Shipwreck Coast National Marine Sanctuary?"

"Absolutely. I've got friends who are archaeologists checking one of the wrecks out, and I'm probably going to write a story about the sanctuary."

"Well, seems like Ben heard some rumors about something nefarious going on with it."

"Any idea what?"

"Max's being vague, of course, but from what I'm gleaning, and what I know of Ben, I'm betting somebody's doing something they're not supposed to."

"Now who's being vague?"

"Sorry. Looks like there have been rumors of people pilfering things that shouldn't be pilfered."

"From the shipwrecks?"

"Yeah. There've been reports that some of the more complete ones have shown signs of disturbance, beyond the notoriously shifting sands of the lake."

Alex had a hunch. "Can you ask him if one of those shipwrecks was the S.S. Senator?"

She heard the keys clicking again. "Done. Wow, that was fast. 'I can neither confirm nor deny...', so that's a yes." Alex stayed silent while she thought about it. "You still there?"

"Yes. Sorry. Just thinking. Thanks. That's a start."

"Anytime. Keep me posted, okay? And I'll keep working Max and see if I can get more info. I'll also try to find out who they assign the story to, if they decide to pursue it. Knowing Ben, he inflated the issue so he could have a legitimate reason to be in Sheboygan while you were there. He'd done it before."

Alex sighed. Was she the only one who hadn't seen that Ben really had been stalking her? Too bad that didn't make her look any less like a suspect, considering everything. She thanked Tad and promised they'd get together when she was back in town.

She opened the sliding glass door and stepped outside. Now that she wasn't worried about Ben showing up at her room, she could exit directly to the lawn instead of going out the front and walking down the hall. It still probably wasn't wise to leave her room unlocked, but she needed fresh air, she needed sand, and she needed to hear the waves. As she neared the rocky shoreline, she saw surfers swimming out to the horizon. Alex walked to a pair of white Adirondack chairs and settled into one, kicking off her shoes and burying her toes in the sun-warmed sand. The wind picked up strands of her hair, which was now long enough to blow across her face. Soon she'd be able to pull it back into a ponytail again. Well, maybe not soon, but she now knew it would happen.

Alex focused on a ship in the distance, gazing in the direction of where the Senator was buried. After talking with Cassidy and Reid the night before, Alex had done some reading up on the shipwreck while waiting for sleep to come. It had been an avoidable crash. Back in 1929, both the Senator and the Marquette were barreling through a foggy night, their captains refusing to pay heed to the danger. They got too close and the Marquette and Senator turned into each other. The Senator, carrying hundreds of automobiles, cleaved, sinking to the bottom of the lake. At 420 feet below the surface, the ship, and its cargo, had been lost for decades until the Wisconsin Department of Natural Resources found it in 2015. Now listed on the National Register of Historic Places, it was one of the cornerstone shipwrecks in the sanctuary. Even though it was relatively recent history compared to what Cassidy and Reid normally studied, she could understand why they'd be fascinated with the wreck.

She thought through her conversation with Tad. That collection of Nash autos would be quite the treasure, if someone could get to them and bring them up. *Was that even possible,* she wondered, or *would they oxidize the minute they breached the surface?* She'd have to find out. If someone was 'pilfering' them, as Tad had said, that would be just the kind of story to land Ben a front page byline, and he'd lived for those. Realizing he'd never have another one saddened Alex. No matter what she felt for him, and while last night's encounter had been nothing but anger, fear, and regret, he didn't deserve to die. Not only did she need to find out who killed him to clear her own name, but to make sure he received justice.

Alex had no idea where he'd been staying. If he was working on a story, it was likely he'd booked an AirBnB or VRBO. The paper would only cover part of it, but Ben had 'standards,' he used to say, which had always made her smile since that was the name of his employer. She could ask Tad again, but she knew he had his own beat to cover.

She had another thought. What if she offered to pick up Ben's story? She'd been a talented investigative journalist, had had several of her own front page bylines, and had left on good terms. She wasn't familiar with Max, but that may be a good thing. He wouldn't know about her history with Ben. He might not know, she amended. If she could get this assignment, she'd be able to follow whatever threads Ben had pulled.

Invigorated, Alex wiped the sand off her feet, put her shoes back on, and pushed up from the chair. She marched quickly back to her room, then opened her laptop and searched for an editor named Max or Maxwell on the staff roster. There. She shot a quick text to Tad asking if Max could have known about her and her past relationship with Ben.

Doubtful, he replied, *He's new, hired long after you guys broke up. Why? You going after Ben's story?*

Alex grinned. *Am I that predictable?*

It makes sense. Good luck. Want me to say anything?

No, thanks.

Keep me posted.

Deal.

Alex dashed off an email to Ben's former editor, explaining that she'd been previously employed by the paper and offering links to some of her best articles. She also explained that she'd heard Ben had been working on an important story regarding the sanctuary, and since she was already in Sheboygan and had the experience, she'd be happy to continue his investigation as a freelancer. No need to send another reporter up and worry about all those expenses. Her room was even covered.

She re-read it, checking for tone, spelling, grammar, and typos, before hitting send. Instead of waiting for a reply, she stuffed her laptop into her bag, grabbed her keys, and headed out to the yacht club. With any luck, Ben's car would be there.

It was a short drive to the marina, yet Max had already replied when she parked and checked her email on her phone. *Tentative*, he'd written. *I'll get back to you by EOD.*

A man of few words, Alex thought, thinking Max had obviously been a newspaper man for some time. She wondered what had happened to her old editor. She also briefly wondered what she was getting herself into. There was a reason she'd left that life.

But now she had even more reason to jump back in.

Alex sent another text, this time to Cassidy, who responded quickly. They were on their catamaran, and of course she could stop by. Before heading to the docks, Alex scanned the parking lot. Ben's Hummer, a big hulking piece of machinery that always seemed to dwarf him, was hard to miss. She knew he used to keep a key under the back bumper. He hated carrying them, especially when he was on assignment. He'd always treated his job like he was Sam Spade or some other noir-era private detective. All cloak and dagger. To give him credit, he had been exceptionally good at uncovering people's secrets.

Now it was Alex's turn to uncover his.

Chapter 10

B en had parked at the edge of the lot, apart from other vehicles and away from the road. He always parked like that since he didn't carry his keys. She felt under the back bumper, reaching as far back as her arm would stretch until her fingertips bumped against the case.

Once inside the vehicle, the scent of his cologne smacked her in the face. It had acted as an early warning system when he drew near. She'd always hated that scent, but now she felt a touch of nostalgia, knowing this was probably the last time she'd smell it.

While Ben was paranoid about carrying his keys with him, he was not paranoid about keeping his notes and files stuffed inside his Hummer. She used to tease him that he fancied himself the journalist's Lincoln Lawyer. *Maybe you should drive a Jaguar*, she'd suggested, *then you could be the Jaguar Journalist*. "No way," he'd said. "Too easy for someone to call me a Jerk Journalist." She smiled at the memory, one of their few good ones.

Alex shook it off. She extracted a pair of the gloves Billy had given her earlier, then began rummaging through Ben's belongings. His laptop bag sat on the floor behind the driver's seat, covered by a black blanket. She left it there while opening the center console. Sitting at the top was a linen envelope. Inside were two tickets to the Friends of Wisconsin Shipwreck Coast National Marine

Sanctuary Gala and Ball, an event taking place the next night. The tickets provided confirmation that he was working on something related to the sanctuary. She was itching to open his laptop and check his email, but first she wanted to continue her search.

It didn't turn up much else, except for some protein snack bars and a stash of Red Bull in the back. She gathered the tickets and his computer bag, then locked the door, taking the key with her. The police were going to be searching for his vehicle, and while she'd agreed to cooperate, she also wanted to give herself some time. Detective Stephens might seem nice, but Officer Rourke most certainly didn't, and either way, they both had a job to do.

The catamaran swayed while Alex tapped her fingernails on the counter, wondering what possible pin Ben could have used to protect his laptop. She'd tried his birthday, the date of his first front page byline, the date he received his first Peter Lisigor nomination, and even 110316, which was when the Cubs won the World Series.

"I'm surprised you remember all that," Reid said.

"I didn't have much choice. We celebrated those dates every year. Or, he celebrated them. I was along for the ride, which usually involved pouring a very drunk Ben into an Uber and making sure we got back home."

"Gosh, Alex, the more you tell me about this guy, the less I can believe you broke up with him. I mean, what were you thinking? He sounds like a real catch," Cassidy said.

Alex laughed. "I know. It took me a while, but I finally saw the light."

"Have you tried your birthday?" Reid asked.

Alex bristled. "No. He was far too narcissistic to use any dates that didn't involve him. Even the Cubs win; he'd placed a huge bet on them. That's how he bought his first Hummer."

"What about when you two started dating?"

She didn't want to enter that date, dreading how she'd feel if he'd used that to protect his work. She tapped it in. "Nope." Then she tried the date she broke up with him. That didn't work either. She knew she'd be hitting the limit of attempted tries soon. She entered the date she received her breast cancer diagnosis.

Bingo.

Alex's shoulders sagged. Of all the dates that meant something important to Ben, she couldn't believe that was the one, especially since that diagnosis is what had ultimately led to her ending their relationship. She was sure there was some big psychological revelation she should be having, but at the moment, she couldn't grasp it. Instead, she focused on figuring out what he'd been working on so she could find his killer.

She cleared her throat and opened Outlook, deciding to start with his emails. She searched for his editor's name and several threads appeared, including one with a subject line about the tickets to the gala. She clicked through the link. Cassidy and Reid had joined her on the bench, and all three of them focused on the screen. "That's the gala we were thinking about attending," Cassidy said.

"We weren't sure if William had any plans for Thursday night and wanted to keep it open," Reid explained.

"He's spending the evening with Billy," Alex said. "One last night of quiet before the chaos, he said."

"Then I think we've got our plans for tomorrow night. Three tickets? Or four?"

"Just two," Alex said, pulling the envelope out of Ben's bag. "I found these. Ethan should be here soon so I'll see if he wants to join me." Her phone buzzed. "Speak of the devil. Excuse me for a moment." Cassidy scooted to the end of the booth so Alex could get out. She exited the galley and walked to the other end of the boat. Fortunately, the wind had died down so she could hear him. "Hey."

"Hey back," he said. "I just landed in Milwaukee. I've got to pick up the rental car and should be up there in a couple of hours."

Alex exhaled loudly. "Sounds good," she said, her voice tight, then gave him her room number.

"Everything okay? You sound tense. Is William being too William?"

Alex laughed. "No, William is being exactly as much William as he should be. I'm—listen, can I tell you about it when you get here?"

"Sounds mysterious, but sure. As long as you're okay."

"I am. I'm with Cassidy and Reid now; they're the archaeologists I told you about. But I'll be back in my room by the time you get here." She hesitated. "I'm looking forward to seeing you," she said softly.

"Same here."

Alex could almost hear the smile in his voice. She hadn't realized how true her statement was until that moment. She'd met Ethan four months before in North Carolina and had seen him again in August, that time in Montana. There'd been a spark, but Alex still wasn't sure if she was ready to see if there was anything more. Still, she'd felt a thrill when William had told her he'd be inviting the attorney. She also knew her incorrigible friend was playing match-maker, but she let it slide.

She hung up and went back to the galley. Cassidy and Reid had scooted together, so close their arms and legs touched, and were browsing Ben's laptop. Alex sat down next to them and saw they'd opened a folder titled SSS. Cassidy picked up the envelope containing the tickets. "I know now why he had these."

"And why we definitely need to be there tomorrow night," Reid said. "Did you tell Ethan?"

"Not yet. I wanted to wait until I saw him." Alex scanned the file Cassidy had opened. Ben had definitely been on to something. "Do you have a printer?"

They did, so Reid got up to get a USB drive and copied the files. He wanted to leave as little trace as possible that they'd been looking through the dead man's computer, and that meant he didn't want to install their printer. He forwarded several emails, then went into the Send folder and deleted them. "That won't fool any computer forensics person worth their salt, but we may be able to hold them off until we've found something substantial, or at least someone who makes a more viable suspect than you. It'd probably be a good idea to put his laptop back in his car on your way out."

Alex nodded. She'd already been planning on it, but she'd also decided to keep Ben's key. She didn't want to make it easy for them.

Evening was quickly approaching and Alex knew the police would be looking for Ben's vehicle and his hotel, or wherever he'd stayed, so she quickly gathered everything and promised Cassidy and Reid she'd call them the next morning.

"Not too early," Reid said. "We're going to have a late night."

"More like a super early morning," Cassidy corrected. "Better if you don't know," she said to Alex cryptically.

Alex gave her a questioning look, but decided to let it go. She left the catamaran, pleased at how quickly she got her land-legs back this time. She was lost in thought as she walked towards the parking lot, then turned the corner. Drats. Ben's Hummer was blocked in by two police cruisers. Alex hesitated for a moment before turning towards her own vehicle, hoping they wouldn't see her. She had Ben's laptop bag; now what was she going to do? She couldn't put it back with the police there. She'd have to find some way to hide it, because once they searched his car and wherever he was staying and came up without a computer, they'd have to know someone had taken it. She just hoped they didn't figure out it was her before she found the evidence she needed to clear her name.

Chapter 11

Ethan spun the cocktail stirrer in his drink, lazily swirling the clear liquid. "I can't believe you spoke to Detective Stephens without an attorney present."

Alex huffed. "Please don't. I know I shouldn't have, but this has been a little hard, you know? And after we found the tracker..."

He reached over and took her hand. "I know. I'm sorry. That was cold of me. You trust her, though?"

"As much as I can. Billy trusts her, so that helps."

Ethan nodded thoughtfully. "And we're going to a fancy-schmancy ball tomorrow night?" When she nodded, he grinned. "So that means I get to see you all dressed up twice this week. Although," he said, leaning forward, "you'd look absolutely beautiful in a canvas bag."

"Hopefully I'd also look good in an orange jumpsuit, since I may be wearing one of those soon."

"Not a chance. You didn't do it and you've got, let's see if I remember everyone: William, Billy, Evelyn, Juke, Cassidy, Reid, and, hmm, wait a minute. I'm forgetting someone. Oh yeah, and me."

Alex smiled. "When you put it like that... Thanks, again, for coming. I know you've been busy with Sergio's co-op."

Ethan waved it off. "I'm just reviewing the paperwork. He's got everything handled. Speaking of Sergio, I forgot someone else. Will Emily be here for the wedding?

"Absolutely. She said she'd close down *Elements* if she had to, because there was no way she'd miss this wedding." Alex smiled at the thought of her neighbor and her on-again, off-again relationship with Sergio. With Emily in Chicago and Sergio in Asheville, their relationship was challenging from the distance alone. Add to that the fact that Emily had a successful restaurant and Sergio an equally successful brewery, restaurant, and nonprofit, and it was amazing they saw each other at all. Alex knew what that was like. She had met Ethan when Sergio'd gotten into a scrape at a festival he'd hosted. Ethan had even helped William when they were in Billings a few months before. Alex still didn't know if she was ready to take another step with the attorney, however, and that was even more in question now, considering what had happened with Ben.

They finished their cocktails, and after Ethan charged them to his room, walked a few blocks to a prohibition-era themed Italian restaurant. On the way, Alex noticed a used bookstore and immediately plastered her face to the window, but it was already closed for the day. That was probably a good thing; if it had been open, they wouldn't have been able to linger over antipasto, truffle gnocchi, and tiramisu while catching up on the past couple of months. Ethan lived in the Asheville area, not too far from Sergio's brewery, but he also had a cabin in Red Lodge, Montana. He'd closed it up for the season in August, shortly after she'd seen him last.

It was a lovely dinner, and around the dessert course, Alex realized it was the first time she'd sat down for a full meal with him. The time flew by, and for a few hours she focused on enjoying their conversation and thinking about how happy she was for William. It wasn't until they walked back to the resort and they neared the entrance that the tension and fear returned. She briefly considered inviting Ethan to her room, but decided that probably wouldn't be the best decision. Not only wouldn't it look good if Detective Stephens were to find out, but she'd also decided to review the files from Ben's laptop since she still had it. However, she could extend the evening, at least a little longer.

"Care to walk by the lake for a little bit?" she asked.

Ethan put his arm around her and drew her in close. "I'd love to," he said, his voice low.

Maybe inviting him back to her room wasn't such a bad idea after all.

Alex put her highlighter down and rubbed her eyes. Despite the temptation, and she had definitely been tempted, she'd decided to retire to her room by herself after their stroll along the beach. The sand had been frigid, with a chilling breeze, so she turned on the fireplace as soon as she got back to her room, alone. She made a cup of chamomile tea, settled into the settee, and began reading.

Almost all the files they'd found on Ben's computer were related to the disturbances of the shipwrecks, as well as more detailed information about each. There was also a profile of Quentin Chase, a wealthy philanthropist who was the biggest donor to the Friends of the sanctuary. After her years as an investigative reporter and her recent run-ins with several men who fit the same profile, Alex was instinctively distrustful that Chase had altruistic motives.

It seemed Ben had been as well.

She opened the browser on her phone and checked the website for the event. There, at the top of the agenda, was Quentin Chase, CEO of Quentum Corp. He'd be giving the opening remarks before introducing Dr. Celeste Moore, the director of the sanctuary. There would be entertainment, a short film about the shipwrecks and the plans for the sanctuary, and a silent auction. Pretty much your standard fundraiser, she thought, complete with lots of people wearing well-tailored suits and shoes that cost more than a round-trip ticket to Paris. She got up and walked to the closet, eyeing the standard black cocktail dress she always packed, just in case. *Would it do?* she wondered. It would have to. Unless... Cassidy was taller than Alex, but she knew the woman attended galas and museum exhibit openings all the time, so she probably had a closet full of gowns. Then again, she did live on a boat, so her wardrobe might be limited. *I'll deal with it in the morning.*

Alex went back to the couch and opened Ben's laptop. Reid had printed out the files on the S.S. Senator, but there had been other documents they hadn't had time to review. While the potential theft of items from shipwrecks was wrong, and definitely worthy of investigation, it didn't seem juicy enough for Ben. He liked his stories to be on the extreme end where drama was concerned. It hadn't been enough for there to be theft; it had to be the biggest theft in decades. It had to be something he felt only he could uncover. It had to be worthy of a Pulitzer Prize.

Stealing items from the bottom of the lake, even though the ships were protected in a national sanctuary, didn't seem egregious enough for Ben. She continued to browse his computer, opening file after file. *There*, she thought. *That's the story he was after*. She opened her own computer so she could send a quick email to Max, Ben's former editor and, she realized, her current one.

That thought made her pause. *What was she doing?* She'd been out of that world for years, and she certainly didn't want to get back in. Did she? The lump in the pit of her stomach, the rising anxiety at the base of her throat, told her no, absolutely not. She would find out who killed Ben, file this one story, and that would be that. She typed out the subject line:

This is what Ben was really working on, isn't it?

Alex sent a brief summary of the file she'd found. It had been filled with all the elements that would have gotten Ben's reporter juices flowing: intrigue, consummate greed, and crisis. If he was right, someone would have had plenty of motive to silence him before he could prove his suspicions.

She grabbed her legal pad and drew a grid. This was an exercise she and William had perfected as they'd had to solve murder after murder. At the top, she wrote column headers for Suspect, Means, Motive, and Opportunity. Then she wrote the first name: her own.

Chapter 12

A knock on the door interrupted Alex as she prepared to make her second cup of coffee. She pushed the button to get it started, then opened the door.

"Surprise!" said Cassidy, beaming, a garment bag folded over her arm.

Alex stared at her. "How did you know?"

Cassidy shrugged. "A good guess. I figured when you packed, you weren't planning on attending a gala, and I can't imagine you travel with a cocktail gown just in case."

Alex realized she was blocking the door while Cassidy stood in the hallway. She stepped back to invite her into her room. "Actually, I do, but it's the same one you saw in Gulf Shores."

"Ah, I remember. Let me guess; that's your standard just-in-case dress?" Cassidy put the garment bag on the bed and began unzipping it. "Don't get me wrong, you looked lovely, but even if you did bring it, I think tonight you should wear something a little more..."

"Gala-like?" Alex asked. "I had the same thought, actually, and was going to mention it when I called you this morning."

"Beat you to it!" Cassidy said brightly.

"I thought you said not to call you too early? Something about being busy this morning?"

Cassidy brushed it off. "We got back sooner than I thought we would," she said cryptically. Alex's curiosity was killing her; she had a hunch the couple had found something important during their early morning, whatever they were doing.

"I realize I'm a little taller than you," Cassidy continued before Alex could ask any questions, "but I thought these might work, and any will work with black heels." She pulled out three cocktail dresses, one that was full-length and two shorter. All three were lovely, but Alex immediately gravitated towards the longer gown. The material, a rich blue so deep it was almost black, was embroidered with silver threads. As she picked up the gown to hold it in front of her, light danced on crystals embedded in the fabric.

It had long sleeves and a high neck, meaning Alex's scars from her cancer surgeries would be hidden, as well as the bruises from Ben's assault. She went into the bathroom to try it on. The cool silkiness of the material fitted her perfectly. Alex particularly liked the slit that nearly reached the top of her thigh. It was a touch long, but with high enough heels, she could get away with it. She came back out into the hotel room.

Cassidy caught her breath. "Perfect. I swear, it looks better on you than it does on me."

"I doubt that."

Cassidy circled her, flicking the skirt to see where it fell on the ground. "You're curvier than I am, so you fill it out better. Means it's not as long as I'd feared. Did you bring shoes?"

Alex pulled out a pair of heels made of sheer nude fabric with rhinestone embellishments.

"Smart color. Goes with everything."

"I've learned to pack lots of neutrals. And shoes with cushioned soles." Alex put the heels back in the closet and hung the gown.

"Thank you so much for bringing this. I promise not to spill anything on it."

Cassidy waved her hand. "Consider it yours. I've got dozens, and like I said, it looks better on you. Now, let's get down to business. What else did you find?" She eyed the table in front of the couch, which was covered with both Alex's and Ben's laptops, the files about the shipwreck, and a notebook.

Alex frowned. "Ben was definitely looking into the Senator, but I don't think that's what got him killed."

Cassidy crossed the room and sat on the couch. She leaned over and picked up Alex's notebook. "May I?" she asked, a little belatedly. When Alex nodded, she started reading her notes. "No offense, darlin', but I thought my chicken scratches were bad. I think I've got the gist of it, though."

"Ben was definitely on to something. So, are you free for a little bit?"

"I could be. What's up?"

"A protest about threats to the lake's ecosystem. The protesters are accusing certain companies of putting the water—and a lot more—at risk. I think that's where we'll get some answers."

"Count me in."

Alex stopped in her tracks. A woman she recognized from her days at the Standard stood three feet in front of her. The other reporter had been an intern at the time, cutting her teeth on the city beat. Alex approached her, ready to give her a hug. "Hey, Serena! It's so good to see you!"

Serena turned. As soon as she recognized Alex, she scowled. Alex dropped her arms, feeling awkward. She scanned the banners tied to fences around the perimeter of the park. A man stood on the stage, speaking into a microphone about the rising pollution levels of Lake Michigan. "I see you got the environmental beat you wanted. Congratulations."

"It's obvious you've been gone. There is no environmental beat any more."

"What? That's outrageous. With everything that's been happening?"

"Exactly. They don't even know I'm here, but somebody has to cover this." Serena stopped, realizing she'd said too much. She gave Alex a pleading look. "Crap. Please don't tell Ben. He'd be furious if he knew I was here, and I know you're close. He never shuts up about you."

Her comment startled Alex. Had Ben pretended they were still together? She wouldn't put it past him. She didn't know if Serena had been close to him, so Alex spoke gently. "I'm sorry, Serena, it seems you haven't heard. Ben is dead."

Serena's eyes widened in shock. "What? I just spoke to him last week. He was all excited, talking about investigating some big story, but he seemed even more excited he was going to see you. I–I think he planned to propose."

This rocked Alex back on her heels. Had he been that delusional? It would explain his extreme anger at her when she brushed him off. She shook her head. "Serena, I don't know how to tell you this, but I broke up with Ben almost two years ago."

Serena gasped. "You what? That's not possible. And why? He did everything for you when you were, you know."

"Going through cancer treatment? No, I'm afraid he didn't. You look a little pale. Why don't we go sit down?" Alex gestured to a picnic table at the edge of the field and moved towards the young woman.

Serena reared back. "I can't. I'm working."

Her reaction confused Alex. They'd always gotten along, and Alex had taken the young woman under her wing. She'd been happy to see her, and to see she was still working at the paper. It made her wonder what had been said about her in the years since she'd left. She'd honestly never imagined anyone would be saying anything about her; why would they?

Serena seemed to crumple before Alex's eyes. The young woman began crying, but forced herself to stop. She stared at the ground while taking a few deep breaths, then looked Alex in the eyes. "Please forgive me. The news about Ben," her voice hitched, "the news about Ben came as a shock. I see him almost every day except when he's traveling for a story. Usually to wherever you are." The last bit came out like a reprimand.

Ah, now I get it. Ben was a force; Alex remembered when she'd first been hired and met the experienced reporter. He was confident, brash, almost overwhelming. She'd been swept off her feet. It took years before she realized what was underneath that charming exterior, and she had a feeling Serena hadn't gotten to that point. Alex studied her for a moment. "He didn't know you were here?"

Serena sniffled, shaking her head. "No. I'd asked if I could come along as backup. I've gotten to be pretty good; Max even told me I'd make a first rate investigative reporter. Max is Ben's editor," she explained. Alex decided not to let her know she already knew who Max was. "I knew Ben was covering the shipwrecks, but I've been hearing noises about things–bad things–happening in the lake. I thought if I could help him find out what…" She stopped speaking.

Alex gave her a moment. "You've got good instincts. I saw that back when you were an intern." Serena straightened her shoulders a bit at the compliment. Alex swept her gaze around the park, filled with people. There were your standard "granola" types–those who were completely free to be who they were–as well as yuppies (*was that even a term any more?*), women and men who looked like suburbanites, children running around, and a few men wearing button-down shirts and ties. Those last were huddled together near the stage, arms crossed and frowns on their faces. Alex decided to pay attention to what the man with the microphone was saying.

His voice boomed across the open space, raw with urgency. "You think because Lake Michigan looks clear that it's safe? You think just because you can't see the pollution, it's not there? Wake up! Every single day, poisons are dumped into this lake. Plastics—tiny, invisible pieces—are in the water we drink, the fish we eat, the very air we breathe. You're already swallowing it, every one of you. And it's only getting worse.

"Corporations don't care—men like them," he shouted, pointing to the cluster of men off to the side. "They're dumping crap into the water because it's cheaper than doing the right thing. That's right: you're drinking and swimming in the stuff they didn't want to pay to clean up. You're drinking poison because a few companies didn't want to spend the money!

"What happens when we can't drink the water anymore? What happens when nothing's left but poisoned fish and dead plants? That's where we're headed. And let me tell you, once this lake is ruined, it's gone—forever. Just like Clearwater Hill. Remember that place? Remember the cancer? How many people died because of their greed?" he shouted, pointing at the men.

"If you care about your own health, if you care about your kids' future, if you care about anything at all, you have to fight this. We need to stop the poison now, or we're looking at a dead lake—a giant graveyard of plastic, toxins, and broken promises. And you'll be the ones paying the price."

Alex wanted to applaud. "I can't believe there's no more environmental beat," she said. "Do they think this stuff isn't happening?"

"Like he said, they just don't care," Serena said.

"If we don't cover it, who will?"

"We? You don't do this any more, remember? You trot around writing about museums and breweries and inconsequential fluff. You're a sell-out."

Alex stared at Serena, shocked by her vitriol. It was the same thing Ben had said when she quit the paper. She wondered if the young woman resented her. Here Serena was, trying to make a difference, and Ben had ignored her for someone who wrote about happy places. She wanted to snap at her, but she'd just given her some terrible news. Besides, she remembered what it was like to be under his spell. She focused on the seething young woman. "I know it seems like what I do isn't important–"

"It isn't."

"–however, people need escapes. They need joy. They need happy stories just as much as they need to know the underbelly of society, the lengths people will go to for greed or anger. They need us both, Serena." Alex returned her gaze to the stage, then pointedly looked at the cluster of men in their stuffy business attire. As she looked, she realized she recognized one of them from the files on Ben's computer: Quentin Chase. She put a mask on her features so she wouldn't betray herself, but Serena noticed, narrowing her eyes at her.

"Do you know him? Quentin Chase?"

Oh, she's observant. "I know his type," Alex said, avoiding the question. "I take it he's one of the industrialists being taken to task?"

Serena snorted. "By whom? His kind gets away with everything. Including destroying our lake. I can't believe Ben didn't see this, that he was focusing on some stupid thefts from stupid ship-wrecks. *This* is what he should be investigating. *This* is what really matters. And you, all you care about is whether or not your little readers can find a good place to eat or take a little tour."

Alex's patience was nearing its end. If Serena had been less patronizing, less scathing, Alex might have let her know that Ben was working on more than the shipwrecks, and might have let her know she was now working on it, too. Instead, she decided the woman was too hot headed and too upset to be trusted. She'd have to keep an eye on her, though. Serena did have good instincts. That could also put her in danger; if Ben had been killed because of this story, it meant Serena needed to be care-ful. Against her better judgment, Alex decided to warn her. "I understand you're upset, so I'll let that go. However, please be careful, Serena. These are not nice people. In fact, they're quite dangerous."

"Dangerous? Don't you think I know that? Ben's dead, he's dead, and I bet you every byline I ever hope to have that *he* had something to do with it." Serena's voice had risen to almost a shout and she pointed her finger directly at Chase. Although Alex seriously doubted he could have heard Serena, he shifted his gaze and stared directly at her. She glared back. Alex sighed. Whether she wanted to or not, she was going to have to get involved with the young woman before she got herself killed, too.

Chapter 13

"What's this all about?"

Alex turned to see Cassidy next to Serena. She hadn't heard her friend approach over all the commotion. "Cassidy, this is Serena. She's a reporter with Chicago Standard. She'd worked with Ben."

Cassidy's face filled with compassion. "I'm so sorry. Were you working with him on his shipwreck story?"

"No. I'm here for something else. Something much more important."

Cassidy snapped her eyes to Alex, then back to Serena. Alex could tell the young woman's anger surprised her. Cassidy turned her attention to the man on stage. "Good for you. Covering this is one of the most important stories you could take on. People like you can make a real difference."

Serena's shoulders sagged at the other woman's understanding, but then she straightened. "Thank you," she said, with force. "We can't let what they're doing be swept under a rug."

Cassidy caught Alex's eyes, and a silent understanding passed between them. Alex spoke. "Serena, it looks like this is wrapping up. Cassidy and I were going to get something to eat. Would you like to join us?"

"I can't. I need to get over there and talk to those, those greedy vultures."

"Bottom-feeders is more like it. Literally," Alex grumbled.

Cassidy spoke softly, her voice quiet enough that Serena had to focus on her to hear what she was saying. "We've got a better idea."

Serena looked back and forth between the two. Her eyes narrowed. "Better than just going right over and talking to him? He's right there. I won't get this chance again."

Cassidy smiled, but there was no mirth in it. She focused on Chase and his colleagues; with her incisors exposed, she looked distinctly dangerous. Alex loved Cassidy, but she certainly wouldn't want to be on her bad side, not when she looked like that. "Trust us."

Serena focused intently on Cassidy, as if she could see through to her real intentions. If Alex had suggested it, she knew Serena would have refused. Cassidy, however, emanated conviction. It drew you in and you felt fiercer because of it. Serena looked at the stage. A band had replaced the fiery speaker and was finishing up its sound check. Quentin Chase and his entourage lingered. He kept glancing towards Serena, and she stared back. "Fine," she said, without turning away from him.

Serena slumped back in her seat, rocking the booth. Alex was also reeling from what Cassidy had just told them. "So that's what Ben was working on," Serena said. "I knew it. I knew it had to be something more than theft."

"I think that's part of it," Cassidy said. "Part of the urgency for checking out the Senator, and what we hoped was around it, was because of what's happening to the lake. We reached out to our friend Tom, and he told us he was concerned about the increasing levels and the damage they could do."

"Why would that affect the Senator? Isn't it too deep?" Alex asked.

"No. In fact, all those contaminants settle. It'll get worse there faster than anywhere else. And that endangers what we found."

"What's that?" Serena asked.

Cassidy shook her head. "Irrelevant, for your needs." Serena was about to protest, but Cassidy put her finger up and she immediately closed her mouth. Cassidy was about ten years younger than Alex, but Alex felt like she was a child around this strong woman. "I'm assuming you don't have plans tonight?"

Serena looked a little sheepish. "Well, I was going to try to find a way to get into Quentum Corp."

Alex recognized the name of Chase's company and was shocked at the young woman's brashness. "How? Do you realize how dangerous that is?"

Serena's eyes flashed. "I'm not a child. I know you remember me as some dumb intern, but that was years ago. Besides, the place'll be empty. They've got that big fundraiser for the sanctuary tonight. Bunch of hypocrites."

Cassidy winked at Alex, then began tapping on her phone. Alex understood. "Funny you should say that," she said. "Want to go to a ball?"

The young woman slumped again. Alex wanted to coach her that if she wanted to be an investigative reporter, she'd need to be a little more subtle with her bodily reactions. "I can't," Serena whined. "I don't have that kind of money. You know what they pay at the paper."

"Not a problem," Cassidy said, then scooted her phone across the table. "One ticket acquired. Now, I'm assuming you need something to wear?"

Serena gaped at Cassidy. "But why?"

"Because you've got good instincts," Alex answered. "You're passionate. Honestly, you remind me of myself when I was your age." Alex groaned. "Wow. I really sound like an old lady, don't I?"

Cassidy grinned at her. "Well, if the truth fits." Alex lightly punched her shoulder. "Hey, careful. I saw how you punched Ben."

"You did what?!" Serena shrieked.

Ethan held out his arm. Alex reached for it, smiling up at him from the front seat. He handed the keys to the valet and they walked up the short steps towards the arts center. The three-story glass entry was lit up like a Broadway marquee. Spotlights illuminated banners displaying several of the historic shipwrecks. They reached the doors and Alex handed over Ben's tickets, then they deposited her cloak at the coat check.

She rubbed her arms to ward off the chill, wincing as she brushed her bruised flesh. Fortunately, the dress covered the marks, which was another reason she'd chosen that one.

Ethan noticed her reaction. "What's wrong? Are you hurt?"

"It's nothing. Just a little sore where Ben grabbed me."

"He grabbed you? If he weren't already dead..."

Alex glared at him. "Don't you dare, Ethan Wells. I can take care of myself, and I did."

Ethan raised his hands. "You're right. So, what'd you do?"

They passed a server holding a tray of champagne flutes and Alex took two, handing one to Ethan. "I punched him."

Ethan threw back his head and laughed, a full-throated guffaw that caused several people to turn and stare. "Sorry, sorry," he apologized. "She just told a really good joke."

"I love a good joke," a deep voice said, and Alex turned to see Reid behind Ethan, Cassidy at his side.

"I told him I punched Ben."

Cassidy grinned. "You should have been there, Ethan. It was awesome."

"Hey now, let's not glorify violence," Alex admonished her.

"But this is Ben," the three of them chorused.

"Was," Alex corrected. "Was Ben."

They looked appropriately chastened. "You're right," Cassidy said, putting her arm around Alex's shoulders. "That was cold."

"And that's why we're here," Reid said gently. "We're going to find out who killed him, because I'm betting all the key players are present."

Alex scanned the room. She immediately spied Quentin, who was holding court surrounded by women in gowns and men in tuxedos. She recognized a few of them from that morning's protest. A man standing several feet away from the group caught her attention. She almost didn't recognize him; it was the speaker who'd lambasted Chase and his colleagues at the protest. Earlier in the day he'd been wearing a t-shirt and jeans, but tonight he fit in with the rest of the crowd. Even his unruly hair was tamed. The look in his eyes, however, was not.

Another group clustered around a tall woman wearing an emerald floor-length gown. From the research Alex had done, she knew that was Dr. Celeste Moore. One of the men in her circle wore a tweed sport coat with leather patches, the quintessential professor garb. That must be Tom Harris. She'd seen a few emails between him and Ben, but they'd been very cryptic. Alex thought briefly about the laptop. She hadn't had a chance to get rid of it yet and it was still in her room. She'd had the presence of mind to put it, along with her own computer and all the files, in her safe, but she'd feel better if she could get rid of the darn thing. If Detective Stephens decided to arrest her, they'd have access to her room and that laptop would be like a confession.

All those thoughts flashed through her mind in seconds. Ethan was studying her face, but she doubted he could tell what she'd been thinking. She gave him a quick smile, then responded to Reid. "I think you're right. There's Quentin Chase. He appeared frequently in Ben's research."

"And there's Tom," Cassidy said, indicating the man in the tweed jacket, confirming Alex's hunch. "He's helping us work with the sanctuary."

"Bit of a cliché, isn't he?" Ethan said.

Cassidy grinned. "Absolutely. And it's entirely intentional."

"Makes people underestimate him," Reid said. "They see him and think, oh look, it's Doctor Doolittle. Little do they know he's one of the sharpest people I've ever met."

"And one of the best divers. We can't keep up with him and can't get nearly as deep as he can. Basically, you don't want to get on his bad side." Cassidy's words were a warning, but she said them with genuine respect and affection.

"On whose bad side?"

They all turned to see Serena. She shuffled her feet and blushed slightly as they appraised her. "You look wonderful," Cassidy said. "I knew that dress would be perfect."

"Thank you," she said quietly.

Alex could tell she felt awkward. "You know what's great about that dress?"

"What?" Serena eyed her, and Alex could tell she still didn't trust her.

"It's black, which means you won't stand out." Before Serena could make assumptions about Alex's meaning, she continued. "As an investigative reporter, you never want to wear something that people will remember. You look beautiful, and you also blend in. Like Cassidy said, it's perfect."

Serena narrowed her eyes at her. "Your dress stands out."

"Yes, some, but I also have the luxury of being a travel writer. Nobody's going to suspect that I care about anything but fluff and inconsequential things, like spending time with the rich and famous at an expensive fundraiser."

Serena had the good sense to blush again. "I'm sorry. I shouldn't have said that."

Alex waved her hand. "I appreciate the apology. It's nothing I haven't heard before, and I've grown pretty thick skin. Benefit of being so old," she said, then winked at Cassidy.

Ethan laughed. "You're the youngest old person I know. Besides, aren't you in your early fifties?"

"Yes, and proud of it." She scanned the room again. "Here's what I think we should do. Cassidy and Reid, since you know Dr. Moore and the professor, why don't you mingle with them? Ethan and I can go meet Mr. Chase. Ethan looks the part of the wealthy donor."

"As do you," he said. She smiled at him.

"What about me?" Serena asked.

"Why don't you talk with our protester friend? And make it obvious. Don't pull him off to a corner or anything, but speak to him where Chase can see you."

"I thought you said I shouldn't stand out?"

"I have an idea."

Chapter 14

Alex threaded her arm through Ethan's. She was growing increasingly comfortable with the attorney, which unnerved her, as did her attraction to him. A long distance relationship would be challenging. They wouldn't see each other often, although with her job, she had more freedom than most.

Actually, she thought with a grin, getting involved with someone who lived several hundred miles away would mean she'd definitely keep her independence. It could be perfect, similar to William and Billy's arrangement.

"What are you smiling about?" Ethan whispered in her ear.

"Oh, just thinking about William. He's going to be upset he missed this."

"Upset? Why would he be upset? He's spending tonight with Billy."

"I keep forgetting you don't know him well. He loves intrigue, especially if it means protecting someone who's been wronged, and that's how he sees the police's suspicion of me. It's probably eating him up that he's not out trying to solve the crime. I can picture him pouting. Either that, or nagging poor Billy."

Ethan laughed. "Billy does know what he's gotten himself into, right?"

"He definitely knows, and wouldn't have it any other way. I've never seen a more perfect couple."

"I don't know," Ethan said, slowing down and looking into her eyes. Alex's breath caught, but then he shifted to Cassidy and Reid, who had reached the professor and doctor. "They seem pretty perfect."

Alex exhaled, surprised to realize she felt relief that he hadn't suddenly tried to take their relationship, whatever it was, to a whole different level. "Yes, they do. Now, shall we go thank our gracious host for the evening?"

"We shall."

They neared the cluster gathered around Quentin Chase. He must have said something amusing, because they were all laughing, especially a thin man standing right next to him. The man kept his eyes on Quentin, who glanced up and saw Alex and Ethan approaching. "Mr. Chase?" Alex said. "We wanted to thank you."

He eyed her briefly, ignoring her extended hand, but directing his gaze to the people surrounding him until they all left except for the thin man. "Thank me for what?" Quentin asked, ignoring Ethan. "And please. It's Quentin. Mr. Chase was my father."

Alex resisted rolling her eyes, although it took almost everything she had. She held his gaze. "For all the wonderful work you've done for the sanctuary. I heard it wouldn't have happened without you."

Quentin continued staring at her. It made her feel uncomfortable, like she was under a microscope. "Oh, I'm only playing a small part."

"I doubt that," Ethan said, extending his hand. Quentin stared at Alex for a couple more seconds before focusing on Ethan and ignoring his hand as well.

"Mr. Chase doesn't shake hands," the thin man said.

Quentin frowned at him. "Excuse Martin. He gets a little protective at gatherings. Now, scurry on, won't you?"

A look of anger crossed Martin's features, but he dipped his head in acknowledgement and walked away. Alex noted he didn't go far.

"And you are?" Quentin asked Ethan, who introduced them. Quentin turned back to Alex. "Have we met before?"

"No," she said. "I'm from Chicago and am just visiting this week."

"Yes, I'm sure I've seen you." His eyes narrowed. "That's right. You were at the protest this morning." He looked her up and down. "You looked a bit different."

"Protest? Oh yes, that. I was at the park to meet a friend before heading to lunch. What was that all about, anyway?" Alex was the picture of innocence. She could feel Ethan's questioning look.

Quentin stared at her, then shifted his focus to look over her shoulder. "But weren't you with her?"

Alex turned. He was staring at Serena, who was deep in conversation with the man who'd been on stage earlier. Serena had her recorder out and was listening intently. "Her? No. Just a random encounter," Alex said casually. "When my friend arrived, we left. Why, do you know her?" She hoped he wouldn't remember that Alex had actually left with both Cassidy and Serena.

He kept staring at the young woman. His gaze was so intense, Alex was sure Serena would feel it. He finally drew his eyes back to Alex, then seemed to shrug it off, resuming the mask of the consummate host. "I'm afraid not. She seemed rather upset, that's all. I will say, the man she's talking with is distinctly unpleasant."

"You know him?"

Quentin's eyes narrowed again. "You certainly have a lot of questions."

Alex laughed it off, hoping to disarm him. "Forgive me, Mr. Chase. I'm an inquisitive person. Here's a more appropriate question for tonight's festivities: what piqued your interest in the sanctuary?"

"Yes," Ethan stepped in before Quentin could answer, "I'd love to know what prompted such generosity. I know this is a government project, but I also know things like this wouldn't happen without important men like you."

Even though Alex knew Ethan had intentionally used the word 'men' to ingratiate himself with Chase, it still grated. She had to fight to keep her face pleasant and neutral, just a vapid socialite who looked pretty on the arm of her big strong man.

Ethan's compliment worked, taking Chase's focus off of her and onto him. It allowed her to study him. He was good looking, with salt and pepper hair and a debonair style. She pictured him stretching his arms and pulling his sleeves to expose his cufflinks, James Bond-style. It didn't take much for her to imagine him as one of the spy's notorious nemeses. The more they talked with him, the more she became certain that Chase had something to do with Ben's death.

She couldn't help herself any more. "I am curious about something, Mr. Chase."

"Quentin. Please."

She smiled, willing it to reach her eyes. "Of course. My apologies. What brought you to the protest today?"

For a moment, Alex didn't think he would answer her, but then he smiled. "I would think it's quite obvious." He gestured to one of the banners promoting the sanctuary. "I have a vested interest in what happens off our shores. Protecting these shipwrecks is, shall we say, a passion of mine. And when I'm passionate about some- thing," he said, focusing intently on her, "I make it my business to know everything that's happening with it. Including anything unpleasant." Quentin's eyes shifted, and Alex knew he was looking at the protester again.

"Was he right?" Alex felt Ethan's eyes on her. "About what's happening? About the intentional pollution?"

Quentin directed his attention to her again, then spoke to Ethan. "She is inquisitive, isn't she? You've got your hands full."

"I wouldn't have it any other way," Ethan said, leaning over, his voice low and almost threatening. "I happen to appreciate strong women; they certainly don't scare me like they do so many men."

Alex could almost feel Quentin growl. She was also none too thrilled with Ethan. While she appreciated what he was trying to do, she loathed it when a man tried to fight her battles, and he knew that. She decided to continue her questioning. "I heard you were particularly interested in the S. S. Senator. Those Nash automobiles would be quite the prize, especially if one could bring them up from their watery grave." Inwardly, she smiled. If William had been there, she knew he'd be groaning and would never let her hear the end of it. *Watery grave?* he'd mock. *Who are you, Hawthorne?* She'd grin, they'd banter, and it would be a lovely evening.

"No one is bringing those autos to the surface, Ms. Paige. Do you have any idea how deep they are? They're more than three times deeper than any expert diver could go."

"But it could be done, right?"

Quentin scrutinized her, then leaned in close. "I think it's time for me to speak," he said in her ear.

The words were innocuous, but his demeanor was distinctly unsettling. When he walked away, followed closely by Martin, Alex stared after him and shivered.

"I'm sorry," Ethan said, surprising her.

"For what?"

"I overstepped. You're more than capable—obviously—of dealing with someone like him."

Alex thawed, slightly. "Yes, yes I am."

Quentin's speech was the standard chucklefest of manufactured humility while simultaneously touting what he'd made possible. Alex wanted to zone out, but she knew she needed to pay close attention to what he said. As he spoke about the shipwrecks, his words sounded good. He sounded like he was interested in preserving history and protecting the lake, but she didn't quite believe him and she'd learned to trust her instinct. Although she'd been wrong about people in the past, it had mostly been about specifics; for example, when the person she thought was a murderer actually wasn't, but was definitely guilty of other heinous crimes. She knew as soon as she got back to her room she'd be doing more research on Quentin Chase, and would do a deep dive (pun intended, she thought to herself) into any reference to him on Ben's computer.

He finished speaking and Alex and Ethan found Cassidy and Reid. They were still talking with the professor, although Dr. Moore had left the group because it was her turn on stage. Reid made the introductions, speaking softly so he wouldn't interrupt the director's speech. The doctor finished, and after a round of applause they were able to speak at a normal conversational level.

"Tom and I go way back, don't we, Professor?" Reid said.

"Longer than I care to admit, because if I did, I'd be admitting how old I am."

"So you really are a professor?" Alex asked, amused.

"I just play one on TV," Tom said. "Not really. I adopted this as a costume, of sorts, many years ago. It disarms people."

"And why, pray tell, would anyone need to be disarmed around you?"

Tom laughed, and Reid explained. "Tom here comes across as very 'aw shucks, gee willikers,' but he's one of the foremost experts in underwater archaeology, has the record for the deepest free dive, and is a formidable opponent in chess. Basically, he's both physically and intellectually daunting."

Ethan grinned. "Chess, eh? Maybe we can play a game while I'm here."

"Don't say I didn't warn you," Reid said.

"I take it you're working with these two on their find near the Senator?" Alex asked.

Tom looked at Cassidy and Reid with a touch of surprise, but he quickly masked it. "I'd ask 'what find,' but it seems they've already let you in on their secret."

"Alex has a way of getting people to tell her things they normally would keep private," Cassidy said.

"Tell me about it," Ethan confirmed, and they all laughed.

Alex studied Tom. "How much do you know about what's happening with the lake?"

"You mean with the illegal dumping?" It was Alex's turn to look surprised. "Yes, I see you know about it," Tom said. "It started a few months ago. Cassidy told me you were at the protest this morning?

Alex nodded. "Briefly. We didn't hear much. I learned more about it from the research a colleague of mine had done."

"You must mean Ben," Tom said. "Reid told me what happened. I'm sorry. Especially for the trouble it seems to be causing you."

"Yes, that's why it's so important I figure out what's really happening. I certainly know I didn't kill him, and with what he'd been uncovering, at least one person here has some serious motive."

Tom turned his attention to the stage. Dr. Moore stood in front of it talking with Quentin. She towered over him, yet she seemed cowed by the shorter man. "At least I know of one person who wouldn't have a motive."

"Celeste? True. She'd be the last person to want anything to happen to the sanctuary," Reid said.

"Despite being Chase's head of R&D. Her innovations in nanocoating are the foundation for making deeper and deeper dives possible. Only problem is, if the byproducts from the process aren't disposed of properly, they can cause cancer," Tom explained.

Alex remembered something from that afternoon. "Like in Clearwater Hills?"

Tom nodded. "The incidences of bladder cancer–a very specific type of cancer, by the way–exploded in that small town once Quentum Corp opened a facility there."

"Was Dr. Moore there when that happened?"

Reid shook his head. "No. My understanding is she didn't start working for him until he moved here."

"And now it's happening again," Tom grumbled. "Those same chemicals are showing up in the lake. And then he donates a gazillion dollars to the sanctuary and she suddenly has the top job. It feels... manufactured."

"But I thought you said she's not a suspect, that you were working with her," Alex said.

"I am, and I don't think she's responsible, but there are certainly a lot of people who'd want to make it look that way."

Alex studied him. "It seems like you know something specific."

Tom tore his eyes from the doctor. "When you rely on people with his kind of money and power, being cynical comes with the territory, I suppose."

Alex nodded. Despite Tom's insistence that the director wasn't a suspect, Alex mentally added her to the list. "If you'll excuse me, I think I'll go ask Dr. Moore a few questions."

They all looked at her with alarm, except for Cassidy, who laughed. "Close your mouths, you three. You look ridiculous." She smiled warmly at Alex. "Go do your thing."

Chapter 15

As Alex walked off, she heard Cassidy explaining to Tom in more detail about Alex's unique ability to get people to open up. It wasn't something she'd ever been able to pin down, and she hoped she still had that special touch, whatever it was. She paused as Dr. Moore walked away from the group she'd been speaking with and headed directly towards her. Alex realized she was standing between the director and the bar, so she was probably on her way to get a drink. When she reached her, Alex turned to walk with her. "Hello, Dr. Moore. I just wanted to say what a wonderful event this is. Your plans for the sanctuary are going to completely bring to life the history of commerce and shipping in the Great Lakes."

"Thank you, Ms..."

"Paige, Alex Paige," she said, thrusting out her hand. "I was on my way to see if I could ask you some questions, but you look like a woman on a mission. May I buy you a drink?"

The director laughed. "How could I say no to that? Sure, let's walk and talk."

Fresh cocktails in hand, the two women stood to the side of the bar so they'd be out of the way. Alex explained that she was a travel writer and that she appreciated Dr. Moore's plans for visitor centers at towns along the stretch of the sanctuary. "Those should be a big tourism draw."

"We certainly hope so. We have some real treasures off our coast. Highlighting them has been a long time coming."

"Was this something you always wanted to do?" Alex asked.

Dr. Moore nodded. "Oh yes, but, like many, I got sidetracked along the way."

"I heard you headed up Research and Development at Quentin Chase's company."

The director frowned, but quickly covered it with a smile. "Yes, that was the part of my path where I got sidetracked. However, it ended up being for the best. Quentin recommended me for this job."

"That's surprising; wasn't he concerned about losing you?"

"I still act as a consultant, and it's a good thing I do. Someone has to keep those corporate types honest. Otherwise, they'll just do whatever makes the most profit."

Alex detected bitterness, or anger, or both, in the doctor's tone. This surprised Alex. "But isn't R&D separate from disposal? I'm sorry; I'm not sure of the correct terminology."

Dr. Moore waved it off. "I made it my business to know how to dispose of the byproducts properly. I wanted to, and want to, make the world a better place. Now I have that opportunity."

The director was not what Alex expected. When she heard about her previous position in Chase's company, and that she got the job after he had recommended her, Dr. Moore immediately became a suspect. But Alex didn't believe she was faking her passion, although the hostile undercurrent confused her. "So he's kept you on as a consultant? What does that entail?"

"Right now, not much. With the launching of this sanctuary, I've barely had time to take a shower, let alone make sure they're doing what they're supposed to do." Dr. Moore sobered. "And now the heavy lifting really begins, but I'm going to have to make the time. I know people like Quentin, and they'll do whatever they can to increase their bottom line."

Alex had more questions, hoping to get to the reason for the doctor's demeanor, but an austere-looking woman in a well-tailored pantsuit approached her. "Celeste, you agreed to an interview with someone named Serena?"

"Yes; is it time?"

The other woman nodded curtly. "I sent you a text."

Celeste opened her clutch and pulled out her phone. "I don't have anything from you."

The woman reached out her hand and Celeste handed her the device. "I sent it to the other number."

"I thought we decided I wouldn't use that phone any more."

The whole exchange bewildered Alex. The woman finally noticed her. "Excuse me for the interruption."

Alex introduced herself. "And you are?"

"Lena. Lena Foster."

"Lena handles PR for both the sanctuary and Quentum Corp. Quentin's loaned her to us while we get through these early growing pains," Dr. Moore explained. "Thank you for the drink, and for the conversation. I hope you enjoy the party."

As the director walked away with Lena, Lena Foster, Alex scanned the room and caught Serena's eyes, then gave her an approving nod. Yes, the young woman definitely had good instincts.

Alex turned to rejoin her friends and stopped. The man who'd been speaking at the protest that morning stood in front of her. "Serena told me I should talk with you," he said abruptly.

"Oh? Oh, yes. You were speaking this morning about what's happening in the lake. I take it she interviewed you for the Chicago Standard?"

"That's what she said, but she seems awfully young."

"How old are you? I'm sorry, I didn't catch your name?"

"Wyatt Rayburn. And I don't see how that's any of your business."

Alex smiled. "Exactly."

He gaped at her, then bowed his head in shame. "You're right. I've been around people like Quentin Chase, fighting people like him, for too long. Takes the trust out of you."

"I get it. I was an investigative reporter many years ago, and seeing all that corruption got to be too much."

"Exactly," he said, repeating Alex's word. "What they're doing to our water, to our air, to our land, it's unconscionable, and I can't get people to see how dangerous they are. I just want somebody to listen, to actually pay attention."

Alex thought of her conversation with the sanctuary's director. "Have you talked to Dr. Moore?"

"Her?" Wyatt scoffed. "I can't get past her little gatekeeper."

"Ms. Foster? Yes, she does seem like she'd be challenging."

He grunted. "That's one way to put it. Besides, Quentin Chase has bought and paid for *Doctor* Celeste Moore," Wyatt complained.

"Is she not a doctor?" *Wow, this man was angry.*

He waved her off. "Oh sure, she's got her Ph.D., but she's not a real doctor."

Alex bit back her retort. It's no wonder no one would listen to the man. "I take it Serena interviewed you about the protest?" she asked, trying to get him to focus.

"Yes. She was particularly interested in the illegal dumping."

"If a reporter is interested in reporting it, isn't that a good thing?"

"Definitely, but she seemed more interested in another reporter, not the dumping."

"Was it Ben? Benjamin Ainsworth?"

He narrowed his eyes at her. "How'd you know?"

"Like I said, I used to be a reporter. I worked with Ben, and Serena was an intern when I left."

"I knew she was too young."

"I left the paper many years ago, Mr. Rayburn."

"Whatever. She claimed she was working with Ben, but then how come she acted surprised that he's dead?"

Alex sighed. She really, really wanted to walk away, but this last statement meant Serena had feigned her ignorance for some reason, and Alex would have to continue talking to him. "How did you find out?"

"He was supposed to meet me at the yacht club Tuesday night. Never showed up. I waited for him for two hours. Wasted my whole night. I went back in the morning and the cops had the docks closed down. One of 'em told me some journalist had washed up on the breakwater. Figured it had to be him. He seemed the kind somebody'd want to kill."

Alex held back her reaction to his callousness. "That had to be frustrating," she managed to say. "I bet you were going to show him proof of everything you've been trying to warn people about."

"You got that right. I got there at 7 p.m. on the dot. He said we'd blow this wide open."

"Why did you wait for him for so long?"

"He sent me a text saying he was on his way, but he had something to take care of first. Believe me, if it weren't so important, I wouldn't have stuck around. Wish I'd known he was probably already dead."

Alex winced. Not only at Wyatt's words, but also at the realization that Ben was late because he'd been stalking her. He must have used the tracker he'd planted to follow her. She shivered, wishing she could get away from Wyatt. But not yet. "Well, you're in good hands with Serena."

He looked at her in shock. "Her? I can't give this to her. It's too important."

Alex leaned in. "Because she's young? Or because she's a woman?"

He opened his mouth and closed it, then opened it again.

"That's what I thought. Good luck, Mr. Rayburn. You'll need it." She spun on her heel. He grabbed her arm. Alex froze and went dead still. She was really getting tired of men grabbing her. "I suggest you remove your hand from my body immediately, Mr. Rayburn," she said, her voice low.

He must have heard the threat in her tone because he released her and backed away. Alex flipped her hair, refusing to turn around and look at him. Several feet away, she saw Ethan watching from a distance, a bemused look on his face. She smiled at him and strode towards him.

"You're magnificent," Ethan said.

"Oh?"

"You should have seen the look on his face. I don't know what you said to him, but it looked like you scared the pants off of him."

"Good, because if he touches me again, he should be afraid." Alex turned to see the protestor, who was standing in place and watching her. She crossed her arms. "Thanks for not coming to my rescue this time." She meant it.

Ethan shrugged. "I learned. And I knew you knew I was here if you needed me. You didn't seem to." He was also watching Wyatt. "Looks like he's going to try to make amends."

The protestor walked towards them, holding Alex's eyes. He reached her and Ethan and held out his hand. Alex ignored it, and he put it down. "I hope you'll accept my apologies. I just get excited."

"No, I don't. That's not much of an apology, and your behavior was reprehensible."

Wyatt had the good sense to look abashed. "You're right. I *am* sorry. I just, I feel helpless. Ben was supposed to help stop this, and now I don't know what to do."

"Yes, you do," Alex said. Her tone was as unforgiving as her words.

For a brief moment, he looked confused. Then he realized what she was implying. "Her? You think I should trust her? You don't think I'll be wasting my time?" Alex simply stared at him. He raised his hands in surrender. "Fine. But you realize these are dangerous people, right? I'm just trying to protect her."

Alex laughed. "No, you're not. You're infantilizing her." She was surprising herself with her unwillingness to brush over this man's behavior, and she could feel Ethan's eyes on her. "If you really want to stop them, you know what to do. Now, if you'll excuse me." Alex took Ethan's arm. "Mr. Wells, I think it's time to leave."

As Alex walked off, she heard Cassidy explaining to Tom in more detail about Alex's unique ability to get people to open up. It wasn't something she'd ever been able to pin down, and she hoped she still had that special touch, whatever it was. She paused as Dr. Moore walked away from the group she'd been speaking with and headed directly towards her. Alex realized she was standing between the director and the bar, so she was probably on her way to get a drink. When she reached her, Alex turned to walk with her. "Hello, Dr. Moore. I just wanted to say what a wonderful event this is. Your plans for the sanctuary are going to completely bring to life the history of commerce and shipping in the Great Lakes."

"Thank you, Ms…"

"Paige, Alex Paige," she said, thrusting out her hand. "I was on my way to see if I could ask you some questions, but you look like a woman on a mission. May I buy you a drink?"

The director laughed. "How could I say no to that? Sure, let's walk and talk."

Fresh cocktails in hand, the two women stood to the side of the bar so they'd be out of the way. Alex explained that she was a travel writer and that she appreciated Dr. Moore's plans for visitor centers at towns along the stretch of the sanctuary. "Those should be a big tourism draw."

"We certainly hope so. We have some real treasures off our coast. Highlighting them has been a long time coming."

"Was this something you always wanted to do?" Alex asked.

Dr. Moore nodded. "Oh yes, but, like many, I got sidetracked along the way."

"I heard you headed up Research and Development at Quentin Chase's company."

The director frowned, but quickly covered it with a smile. "Yes, that was the part of my path where I got sidetracked. However, it ended up being for the best. Quentin recommended me for this job."

"That's surprising; wasn't he concerned about losing you?"

"I still act as a consultant, and it's a good thing I do. Someone has to keep those corporate types honest. Otherwise, they'll just do whatever makes the most profit."

Alex detected bitterness, or anger, or both, in the doctor's tone. This surprised Alex. "But isn't R&D separate from disposal? I'm sorry; I'm not sure of the correct terminology."

Dr. Moore waved it off. "I made it my business to know how to dispose of the byproducts properly. I wanted to, and want to, make the world a better place. Now I have that opportunity."

The director was not what Alex expected. When she heard about her previous position in Chase's company, and that she got the job after he had recommended her, Dr. Moore immediately became a suspect. But Alex didn't believe she was faking her passion, although the hostile undercurrent confused her. "So he's kept you on as a consultant? What does that entail?"

"Right now, not much. With the launching of this sanctuary, I've barely had time to take a shower, let alone make sure they're doing what they're supposed to do." Dr. Moore sobered. "And now the heavy lifting really begins, but I'm going to have to make the time. I know people like Quentin, and they'll do whatever they can to increase their bottom line."

Alex had more questions, hoping to get to the reason for the doctor's demeanor, but an austere-looking woman in a well-tailored pantsuit approached her. "Celeste, you agreed to an interview with someone named Serena?"

"Yes; is it time?"

The other woman nodded curtly. "I sent you a text."

Celeste opened her clutch and pulled out her phone. "I don't have anything from you."

The woman reached out her hand and Celeste handed her the device. "I sent it to the other number."

"I thought we decided I wouldn't use that phone any more."

The whole exchange bewildered Alex. The woman finally noticed her. "Excuse me for the interruption."

Alex introduced herself. "And you are?"

"Lena. Lena Foster."

"Lena handles PR for both the sanctuary and Quentum Corp. Quentin's loaned her to us while we get through these early growing pains," Dr. Moore explained. "Thank you for the drink, and for the conversation. I hope you enjoy the party."

As the director walked away with Lena, Lena Foster, Alex scanned the room and caught Serena's eyes, then gave her an approving nod. Yes, the young woman definitely had good instincts.

Alex turned to rejoin her friends and stopped. The man who'd been speaking at the protest that morning stood in front of her. "Serena told me I should talk with you," he said abruptly.

"Oh? Oh, yes. You were speaking this morning about what's happening in the lake. I take it she interviewed you for the Chicago Standard?"

"That's what she said, but she seems awfully young."

"How old are you? I'm sorry, I didn't catch your name?"

"Wyatt Rayburn. And I don't see how that's any of your business."

Alex smiled. "Exactly."

He gaped at her, then bowed his head in shame. "You're right. I've been around people like Quentin Chase, fighting people like him, for too long. Takes the trust out of you."

"I get it. I was an investigative reporter many years ago, and seeing all that corruption got to be too much."

"Exactly," he said, repeating Alex's word. "What they're doing to our water, to our air, to our land, it's unconscionable, and I can't get people to see how dangerous they are. I just want somebody to listen, to actually pay attention."

Alex thought of her conversation with the sanctuary's director. "Have you talked to Dr. Moore?"

"Her?" Wyatt scoffed. "I can't get past her little gatekeeper."

"Ms. Foster? Yes, she does seem like she'd be challenging."

He grunted. "That's one way to put it. Besides, Quentin Chase has bought and paid for *Doctor* Celeste Moore," Wyatt complained.

"Is she not a doctor?" *Wow, this man was angry.*

He waved her off. "Oh sure, she's got her Ph.D., but she's not a real doctor."

Alex bit back her retort. It's no wonder no one would listen to the man. "I take it Serena interviewed you about the protest?" she asked, trying to get him to focus.

"Yes. She was particularly interested in the illegal dumping."

"If a reporter is interested in reporting it, isn't that a good thing?"

"Definitely, but she seemed more interested in another reporter, not the dumping."

"Was it Ben? Benjamin Ainsworth?"

He narrowed his eyes at her. "How'd you know?"

"Like I said, I used to be a reporter. I worked with Ben, and Serena was an intern when I left."

"I knew she was too young."

"I left the paper many years ago, Mr. Rayburn."

"Whatever. She claimed she was working with Ben, but then how come she acted surprised that he's dead?"

Alex sighed. She really, really wanted to walk away, but this last statement meant Serena had feigned her ignorance for some reason, and Alex would have to continue talking to him. "How did you find out?"

"He was supposed to meet me at the yacht club Tuesday night. Never showed up. I waited for him for two hours. Wasted my whole night. I went back in the morning and the cops had the docks closed down. One of 'em told me some journalist had washed up on the breakwater. Figured it had to be him. He seemed the kind somebody'd want to kill."

Alex held back her reaction to his callousness. "That had to be frustrating," she managed to say. "I bet you were going to show him proof of everything you've been trying to warn people about."

"You got that right. I got there at 7 p.m. on the dot. He said we'd blow this wide open."

"Why did you wait for him for so long?"

"He sent me a text saying he was on his way, but he had something to take care of first. Believe me, if it weren't so important, I wouldn't have stuck around. Wish I'd known he was probably already dead."

Alex winced. Not only at Wyatt's words, but also at the realization that Ben was late because he'd been stalking her. He must have used the tracker he'd planted to follow her. She shivered, wishing she could get away from Wyatt. But not yet. "Well, you're in good hands with Serena."

He looked at her in shock. "Her? I can't give this to her. It's too important."

Alex leaned in. "Because she's young? Or because she's a woman?"

He opened his mouth and closed it, then opened it again.

"That's what I thought. Good luck, Mr. Rayburn. You'll need it." She spun on her heel. He grabbed her arm. Alex froze and went dead still. She was really getting tired of men grabbing her. "I suggest you remove your hand from my body immediately, Mr. Rayburn," she said, her voice low.

He must have heard the threat in her tone because he released her and backed away. Alex flipped her hair, refusing to turn around and look at him. Several feet away, she saw Ethan watching from a distance, a bemused look on his face. She smiled at him and strode towards him.

"You're magnificent," Ethan said.

"Oh?"

"You should have seen the look on his face. I don't know what you said to him, but it looked like you scared the pants off of him."

"Good, because if he touches me again, he should be afraid." Alex turned to see the protestor, who was standing in place and watching her. She crossed her arms. "Thanks for not coming to my rescue this time." She meant it.

Ethan shrugged. "I learned. And I knew you knew I was here if you needed me. You didn't seem to." He was also watching Wyatt. "Looks like he's going to try to make amends."

The protestor walked towards them, holding Alex's eyes. He reached her and Ethan and held out his hand. Alex ignored it, and he put it down. "I hope you'll accept my apologies. I just get excited."

"No, I don't. That's not much of an apology, and your behavior was reprehensible."

Wyatt had the good sense to look abashed. "You're right. I *am* sorry. I just, I feel helpless. Ben was supposed to help stop this, and now I don't know what to do."

"Yes, you do," Alex said. Her tone was as unforgiving as her words.

For a brief moment, he looked confused. Then he realized what she was implying. "Her? You think I should trust her? You don't think I'll be wasting my time?" Alex simply stared at him. He raised his hands in surrender. "Fine. But you realize these are dangerous people, right? I'm just trying to protect her."

Alex laughed. "No, you're not. You're infantilizing her." She was surprising herself with her unwillingness to brush over this man's behavior, and she could feel Ethan's eyes on her. "If you really want to stop them, you know what to do. Now, if you'll excuse me." Alex took Ethan's arm. "Mr. Wells, I think it's time to leave."

Chapter 16

"And then she told him he was infantilizing Serena," Ethan laughed. "It was glorious."

William chuckled, shaking his head. "That's my girl."

Alex lightly punched him on the shoulder. "He was a jerk."

"Yes, yes he was," Ethan agreed.

"Do you think he'll take your advice?" William asked.

"What, to talk to Serena? He already has. When we stopped to get my cloak we saw him approaching her."

"You sure it was safe to leave Serena with him? If he grabbed you, what's he likely to do to her?" Billy asked.

"Cassidy and Reid were keeping an eye on her. They'd already planned to make sure she got back to her room safely. I got a text from Cassidy at two in the morning letting me know she was safe and sound."

"Ugh."

"Yes, ugh, but I was glad to hear they'd just left Serena and they'd had a very productive chat." Alex dipped her bacon in the center of her egg. It broke the surface and the bright yellow yolk spread across the plate. She dragged the strip of meat through it and took a bite.

William sighed. "I can't believe we missed all that excitement." Billy scowled at him, and he quickly corrected his statement. "Not that I wanted to be anywhere else but with you, my love." Billy kissed him on the cheek, and all was forgiven.

Alex smiled at the couple. "You know what I can't believe? That you're getting married tomorrow. Are you ready?"

"Absolutely. I've been waiting my whole life for this," William said.

The friends talked about their plans for the day and enjoyed the rest of their breakfast. Alex was going to meet up with Cassidy and Reid at the marina. She hoped to catch up with Serena later, but she knew they'd fill her in on what Rayburn had told the young reporter the night before. She didn't feel like she was any closer to finding out what happened to Ben, although she was becoming increasingly convinced that Quentin Chase had something to do with it. He may not have been the one to kill him, but she thought it was likely. He had the most to lose from Ben's story and the most to gain from his death.

If, she thought, what she was guessing was true.

If Quentin was dumping chemicals into the lake, and Ben had discovered it, he could have destroyed the philanthropist's reputation. It was also illegal, but Alex knew someone like Quentin Chase would most likely get away with fines and a slap on the wrist, which was what happened in Clearwater Hills. No, the CEO wouldn't be worried about the legal repercussions, but his reputation? His standing in the community as the big savior of the sanctuary? Now that was something he'd fight for, especially after he'd worked so hard to rehabilitate his image.

Alex took the last bite of her bacon and put her napkin on the table. "Allright, you lovebirds. I've got to head out." She kissed Ethan on the cheek. "I'll see you tonight at the rehearsal dinner.

Try to keep this one out of trouble," she said, pointing at William with a grin.

"Try to keep yourself out of trouble, Missy. I've got my own personal detective and my own personal attorney. I'll be just fine."

"That reminds me; where are Juke and Evie?"

"With the visitor's bureau. They're seeing how they can coordinate promotion between Alvin's Landing and Sheboygan, especially since boating's such a big deal here."

"Smart. Well, I'll see you later." She stood up and turned to Ethan. "I'm sure everything'll be fine, but could you keep your phone handy today? I'm hoping I won't need you, but if I do..."

"Of course. You can always call me. Anytime."

"Now who're the lovebirds," William said. Alex gave him an exasperated look, then waved goodbye.

The restaurant was right off the lobby. As Alex started to cross the open space to head to her room, she noticed Detective Stephens and Officer Rourke at the reception desk. The detective was speaking to the woman behind the counter and Rourke faced the way Alex had planned to head. *Crap*, she said under her breath. She quickly darted to the right, away from the lobby, then raced down the stairs. Her floor was one below. She ran to her room, pulling her key card out as she went. Since she'd stayed up after getting back from the gala to dig deeper into Ben's research, his laptop and notes were strewn all over the coffee table. She'd also added her own notes, recording as much as she could about Quentum Corp and about Wyatt's protesting activities.

Alex reached her room, touched the card to the pad, and raced in. She grabbed the Do Not Disturb sign and hung it before setting the deadbolt. She scooped up Ben's laptop bag and shoved his computer, as well as hers, her notebooks, and all the files into the bag. She reached the sliding glass door when she heard a knock. "Ms. Paige? Hello, Alex Paige? This is Detective Stephens. We'd like to ask you a few questions." Alex hesitated for just a moment. She took one last glance around the room, spying her phone charger. *Just in case,* she thought, realizing she didn't know when she'd be able to return. She unlocked the sliding glass door and slowly slid it back, being as quiet as possible. The front door rattled, telling Alex that Stephens and Rourke had a key, which meant they probably had a search warrant.

Alex closed the door, glad the resort seemed to keep the tracks clean and well-oiled because it slid smoothly. She hesitated, thinking about which direction the police would take, then went the opposite way. Despite every cell in her body wanting to take off in a run, she knew people would see that and notice, especially when a uniformed police officer began asking questions. Instead, she tried to seem like she was strolling, and she refused to look back. She finally reached the end of the building and rounded the corner, then walked towards the river that flowed into the lake. She followed the walk that bordered the water; it was hidden by the restaurants and shops that attracted tourists. She knew she didn't have much time. She also knew she couldn't take her car. If Detective Stephens had a search warrant for her room, she probably had one for her car, too.

Alex texted Ethan. *Stephens at my room. Pick me up at the bookstore?* She would have preferred to text Cassidy, but Ethan was closer. She just hoped he'd remember the store from their walk from the resort to dinner the other night. She reached the entrance and tried the handle. It didn't budge. It was too early, she realized belatedly. Hopefully it would take some time for the detective to start searching the area. Her phone buzzed.

1 minute.

Alex slipped around the corner of the bookstore, occasionally peeking around. After what was the longest forty-eight seconds of her life, she saw Ethan's black SUV slow down in front of the store. She ran to it, and he'd barely stopped before she jumped in and he took off.

"To the marina?" Ethan asked.

Alex shook her head, trying to think. "No. They'll know about Cassidy and Reid." She stared out the window as he drove aimlessly, then had an idea. "Got it." She sent a quick message to Cassidy. *Change of plans. Garden Club. Bring everything. ASAP.*

Now all she had to do was wait and hope Cassidy understood her cryptic message.

Chapter 17

Ethan sat on the bench while Alex paced around the small parking lot. She barely completed two full circuits before a vehicle pulled in. Reid got out of the passenger side. He immediately walked toward the trail that led to the mounds, but stopped before following it. "There are so many," he said, his voice laced with awe.

"Pretty cool, isn't it?" Cassidy said, joining him. "Makes you wonder how many mounds were there originally."

"I bet that canoe we found was delivering goods to the people who built these."

"Hey, I know this is your thing, but could we focus? Alex is literally running from the police," Ethan said, then lowered his voice. "Against the advice of her attorney."

Alex rolled her eyes. "We've been through this. And just what do you think would have happened if they'd waltzed into my room and found Ben's laptop and notes? Forget questioning; I'd be under arrest right now, and rightfully so."

Cassidy raised her eyebrows.

"If I were Detective Stephens, I'd arrest me." Alex began counting off the reasons on her fingers. "Ben has been stalking me across state lines. We were seen to have a very public argument. I punched him so hard it knocked him down."

"Which was awesome," Reid grinned.

In that moment, he reminded her of William, and Alex couldn't help but smile back at him, but only for a second. "Yes it was. However, since I 'found' his body the next morning," Alex said, using air quotes to highlight the suspicious nature of it, "I'm obviously the most likely suspect. Throw in the fact that I have his possessions and I'd be lucky to get bail. I certainly wouldn't be able to be at the wedding."

"And you think you'll be able to now?" Ethan asked. "They know where you'll be tomorrow, Alex. You can't run forever."

"Which is exactly why we need to prove, today, that Quentin Chase murdered Ben."

"There might be a problem with that," Cassidy said.

"What do you mean?"

"He's got an alibi for Tuesday night. The whole night."

Alex sagged. "Let me guess. Lena. Lena Foster."

Cassidy nodded.

"Could she be lying?"

Reid shook his head. "Serena followed Lena after their interview. She found her in one of the side galleries with Quentin and overheard them. Apparently, she was with him Tuesday night."

"The really disturbing part, Serena said, was that it didn't sound like Lena would have minded if Quentin had committed murder." Cassidy shuddered.

"I knew I didn't like her," Alex muttered. "He could have had somebody else do it. The man's got enough money."

"What about Wyatt Rayburn?" Ethan asked. Alex gave him a questioning look, surprised he was participating, considering how upset he was that she was 'hiding out,' as he'd said. "I still think you should go to the station," he explained, reading her expression, "but since you're obviously not going to do that, we may as well figure this out."

Alex walked over to the beginning of the trail and stared off into the woods. At that moment, she really wished William was with her. Even though she'd been a talented investigative reporter and had a knack for uncovering the truth, that had been years ago, and she'd grown to rely on her quirky friend. He saw things differently than she did, which made them a good pair. But, he wasn't there, and Ethan, Cassidy, and Reid were. She turned back around to face her friends. "Do you think Wyatt made it up? The story about waiting for Ben for two hours?" When they gave her a confused look, she realized they didn't know what Wyatt had told her the night before. She filled them in. "He was pretty mad about it, too. He's definitely got anger issues."

"But what would his motive be?" Cassidy asked. "Wasn't Ben going to help him expose what's happening?"

"Supposedly. That's what Wyatt said, but who knows what Ben was really up to?"

"You've been through his laptop and his files," Ethan said. "What do you think?"

Alex shook her head. "Honestly? I don't know. He was obviously investigating the thefts from the shipwrecks, but he was also looking into the rising levels of pollution. Thing is, he didn't seem to have any proof that anybody was dumping. Maybe..." she paused.

"—maybe that's what got him killed," Ethan finished.

Cassidy and Reid glanced at each other, a look between them a confirmation of something. "Yesterday, when we had to get up super early? It was because Tom had gotten us access to the ROV."

This startled Alex. "What? Did you see something? Why didn't you say anything last night?"

"Because we didn't know then. It wasn't until this morning we were able to really examine the footage." Cassidy nodded at Reid and he walked to their car and retrieved a tablet from the back seat. He handed it to Cassidy and she motioned for Ethan to scoot over. She sat down, then patted the open spot next to her for Alex to join her. Reid moved behind the bench so all four of them could see what Cassidy pulled up on the screen.

At first, the image was dark and murky, but it quickly began to clear. A spotlight from the ROV swept slowly in a semi-circle, barely cutting through the depths. Then something bright flashed.

"What's that?" Alex asked, pointing to the screen.

Cassidy had already paused the video. She zoomed in. Alex gasped when she realized what they were staring at. "That," Cassidy said, "is Wyatt's proof. And would have been Ben's, if he'd been able to take the ROV down there, too." She tapped the screen and the video resumed.

The camera panned across a metal barrel that was partially buried in the sand. It seemed like the seal was intact. At least there wasn't a stream of toxic chemicals escaping, which was a relief. It looked like footage put out by environmental groups to illustrate what happened before passage of the EPA, and was still happening in some places. The light flashed again as the camera reversed its course and swept across the barrel, the reflection from the symbol for toxic waste causing the glare.

The video ended and they stared at the screen. Finally, Alex spoke. "Do you think Ben knew about this?"

Cassidy shrugged. "I don't know. Whoever's dumping chose this spot because it's so deep that it's impossible to get to without the proper equipment, which is prohibitively expensive."

"Not for someone like Quentin," Alex said.

"But why would they dump it near one of the shipwrecks? That just seems stupid, since there's so much work going on with the sanctuary," Ethan said.

Alex agreed with him. "They probably didn't," she mused. "They probably threw it overboard further into the lake, not realizing how much things drift out there."

She thought about the stories of her hometown, and how shifting sands created a large portion of Chicago's shoreline. Most of Grant Park and several acres of the Streeterville neighborhood were created by people dumping trash, which caused the sand to accumulate. One early resident added several thousand acres to his property simply by building a pier. "Or maybe somebody got lazy," she continued, "figuring nobody would ever find it, even with the S. S. Senator right there, because it's too hard to reach."

Ethan reached for the tablet. "May I?" Cassidy handed it to him and he zoomed in. "Gotcha." He turned the screen so they could see Quentum's logo.

"If Ben had found out about this..." Alex began.

"Then Quentin Chase definitely had motive," Ethan said.

Alex checked the time. She had an interview at the art preserve set up in twenty minutes. As much as she hated the idea of it, maybe she could convince Wyatt to meet her there so she could talk to him after completing her interview. She obviously couldn't go back to her room and the museum should be safe. Right now, however, she couldn't go anywhere without Ethan, her de facto chauffeur. "Can you take me to the arts preserve? I've got an appointment with the director."

"You're still going?" Ethan asked, shocked.

"Of course. Detective Stephens doesn't know I'll be there, and I still have to do my job."

"Fine, but keep your phone out while you're interviewing. If Stephens shows up, I'll text you." He frowned. "I can't believe I'm doing this."

"You're not doing anything illegal, Ethan. I haven't been served, and I haven't left town. As far as they know, I'm just out and about."

"You're their primary suspect, Alex," he said, the exasperation obvious. "From what you told me, they obviously got a search warrant for your room."

"They did what?" Cassidy asked sharply. She still sat between them and her head swiveled back and forth.

Alex brushed it off. "It's nothing. I left through the sliding doors. They never saw me and never knew I was there."

"It's *not* nothing," Ethan said.

She could tell he was angry, but Alex had no choice. She had to find out what happened, and she had to do it today. No matter what, she was going to be at William's wedding, and there was no way she'd let anything ruin it. Like, for example, being arrested for murder.

Alex sent a couple of text messages, then got up. She stood in front of Ethan and took his hands. "I have to do this," she said, hoping he'd understand. She still didn't know him very well. She also knew this was a real test of their burgeoning relationship. It was one thing to ask him for legal assistance for someone else, as she'd done in Montana. It was another thing entirely to ask him to help her evade arrest.

Ethan stared her in the eyes. His face was stern. She thought for sure he'd tell her she was on her own. Instead, he stood up and wrapped her in his arms. She sagged, inhaling his evergreen scent.

Chapter 18

Alex stared at the five-foot tall sculpture made entirely of chicken bones. Dozens of works by the same person surrounded her and the director explained the local KFC would save bones for the artist. While the story was fascinating, it was difficult for Alex to concentrate on what the director was saying because she was focused on waiting for texts from Ethan or Wyatt. She also kept looking at the entrance to whatever gallery they happened to be in, concerned Detective Stephens and Officer Rourke would come barging in, handcuffs brandished, at any moment. Good thing she was recording the interview so she could listen to it later. They finally wrapped it up, and Alex explained she wanted to wander the galleries on her own to really get a feel for the place.

She ascended the stairs to the third floor, anxiously checking her phone. As she reached the top step, she finally received a notification that Wyatt was there. She told him where to meet her and walked to the windows overlooking the parking lot.

"This is awfully cloak and dagger, isn't it?" Wyatt said from behind her.

Alex continued looking out the window. "What was Ben supposed to give you Tuesday night?"

"No preamble. Got it. I don't know. He just said he knew who was dumping waste into Lake Michigan."

"Did he say it was Quentum Corp?"

"No. He was burying the lede–that's what you reporter types say, right? Make it a cliffhanger? He would only tell me in person. Also very cloak and dagger."

"Which I imagine you would appreciate, considering the gravity of your accusations."

"My accusations? That sounds an awful lot like you don't believe me, Ms. Paige."

Alex shook her head. It was sad how angry and distrustful he was. She understood, but it was still disheartening to be on the receiving end. "And why should I, Mr. Rayburn? I don't know you, and everything I've seen and heard from you has been vitriol and yes, accusations. I'm trying to find out who killed Ben."

"Oh, so the poisons in our water don't matter to you."

"That is not what I said. Don't put words in my mouth. You know what? Forget it. I thought we could share information and possibly solve both our problems, but I can't do this." Alex turned to walk away.

Wyatt reached his arm out, but wisely stopped before touching her. "You're right. Can we start over?"

Alex sighed. She'd known exactly what would happen if she threatened to halt the conversation: that he'd acquiesce. She knew she was manipulating him, but she didn't have much time and needed to find out everything he knew. And if he was lying about Ben, if Wyatt *was* the one who'd murdered him, at least they were in a public place.

She wished the whole week could start over. She wished she'd ignored Ben altogether and hadn't engaged with him. She definitely wished she hadn't punched him. Despite their issues, which were legion, knowing her last interaction with Ben had been to hit him in the face was something she'd regret for a long time.

"Fine. Look, there are trails outside and I could use some fresh air," she said. As they crossed the gallery to the stairs, she put her phone in her back pocket out of habit, forgetting Ethan's admonition.

She descended quickly, her eyes darting to make sure Detective Stephens wasn't lurking. When they reached the bottom of the stairs, Alex shook herself off. "This is getting ridiculous," she muttered.

"What is?" Wyatt asked.

Alex silently cursed to herself. She didn't think she'd spoken loud enough to be heard. "This cloak and dagger stuff, as you put it. I wish I could simply believe the police are doing their job."

Wyatt guffawed. "Yeah, right. Not when a big wig like Quentin Chase is the number one suspect. People like him get away with everything."

They'd reached the doors, so Alex waited until they were outside and walking towards the path before she spoke. "Oh, you haven't heard? I'm their primary suspect."

Wyatt eyed her warily. "Did you?"

"Did I what?"

"Did you kill him?"

"No. Of course not. Not that I expect you to believe me." Alex focused on the path in front of her, swiping errant tree limbs out of her way. Although Wyatt was behind her, she could practically hear him shrug.

"Doesn't matter to me. Except somebody, maybe you, killed him before I could find out what I needed to know."

Alex stopped. She hung her head, then turned to face Wyatt with her hands on her hips. "Look, I don't know how we got off on the wrong foot, but I'd like to start over." She thrust out her hand. "Hi, I'm Alex Paige. I'm a travel writer and former investigative reporter. I care about our environment. I love Lake Michigan. I want to find out who is dumping the crap that's killing the lake and, by extension, us. I also want to find out who killed Ben Ainsworth. And, I would like to clear my name. Would you be interested in helping me do these things?"

Wyatt studied her, then grinned. He shook her hand vigorously. "I'd be delighted."

Alex shook her head at his instant transformation. The man was exasperating. "Great. Now, do you have any suggestions? Because I'm out of ideas and I'm running out of time."

"Police hot on your trail, eh?"

"You could say that." Alex didn't want to explain about William's wedding. She felt like she'd just made a breakthrough with Wyatt, but she didn't want to get too close. The man's mercurial nature made her doubt he was completely trustworthy.

Wyatt checked his watch, an old school Swatch. Alex hadn't seen one of those in twenty years. "We need to leave now."

"Why?"

"Because I know where Chase will be, and if we want to catch him, this is the time."

They walked back to the parking lot and Alex made her way to the driver's side of Ethan's car. "Wyatt's got a lead, so I'm going with him."

"You're what?"

She could tell he was upset, and she realized she was being rude after everything he'd been doing to help her. "I'm sorry," she said, more gently. "I appreciate your help, I really do, but this is something I have to do."

"You barely know the guy."

"I barely know you," she said, taking the edge off her words with a smile, "but I know what you mean. I need to do this."

"Do you trust him?"

"Wyatt? No. The man's moodier than winter in Chicago. But he's been following Quentin Chase for a while. And now that we know for a fact his company is polluting the lake—"

"We don't know for a fact that he's the one responsible," Ethan protested. "Anybody from his company could have dumped that barrel."

Wyatt tapped on his horn and Alex wanted to scream. Stuck between two impatient men, she'd had about enough of both of them. She turned to Wyatt and put her hand up, palm out, telling him to wait. Then she turned back to Ethan. "Now you're just being obstinate." She took a deep breath. "Listen," she'd said, "this is not your call. I appreciate everything you're doing to help, but I don't have any other option."

"Sure you do. You could talk to Detective Stephens."

Alex laughed. "I thought you were supposed to advise me not to talk to the police."

"I am. You just get me flustered," he huffed.

That was the wrong thing to say. Alex hated it when someone justified their behavior by saying it was someone else's fault. She'd dealt with enough of that when she was with Ben. Her voice chilled. "Thank you, again, for everything, but I'm doing this."

Ethan glared at her, then his gaze softened. "Fine. But keep your phone handy."

"I will."

"Where are you going?"

"Better you don't know."

"Seriously?"

"Ethan, you're an attorney, and if there *is* an arrest warrant out for me, you can't be seen as harboring a fugitive. The less you know, the better."

"Do you realize how infuriating you are?" he muttered.

Alex smiled, then leaned down into the car and kissed him on the cheek. She walked away without a word.

Chapter 19

The restaurant buzzed with conversation as Alex waited with Wyatt at the host stand. She glanced around the nearly full dining room and almost immediately saw Quentin sitting in a booth with a woman sitting across from him. Alex assumed it was Lena, Lena Foster. In the booth in front of them, Alex was startled to see Serena sitting by herself, and it was obvious she was trying to eavesdrop on the couple behind her. Alex excused herself and bade Wyatt to follow her, then she threaded her way towards the young woman. She slid into the booth without waiting for her to notice her. "Ahem," she cleared her throat.

Serena glanced up sharply, her eyes widening as she realized it was Alex and that Wyatt was there as well. She leaned forward. "What are you doing here?" she hissed.

"Same thing you are." Alex said. Wyatt sat next to Serena, forcing the young woman to scoot over. Alex felt her phone vibrate and pulled it out of her pocket.

I still don't think this is a good idea.

Alex rolled her eyes. *You made that very clear.* She knew Ethan was mad at her, but she wasn't exactly happy with him. The whole exchange didn't bode well for their prospects, but she also knew this was an unusual circumstance.

"Are we disturbing you?" Wyatt said, pointing at her phone and leaning over so he wouldn't be heard by the people sitting behind him.

Alex frowned at him, but she started to put her phone back in her pocket. It buzzed again. Another text. She ignored it, turning her phone completely silent so it wouldn't even vibrate. She focused on Serena. "Have you learned anything?"

Serena shook her head, also bending over the table. "Not yet," she whispered. "She's pushing something about Belize and he's blowing her off. Wait." She paused, listening intently. Her eyes widened.

Wyatt stretched, angling his head towards the back of the booth. "No way," he said.

Alex couldn't hear a thing. "What? What's happening?"

Wyatt and Serena both glared at her and put their fingers to their lips. "Shhh." Then they ruined it by glancing at each other and smirking.

Alex rolled her eyes. She'd had enough of both of them. "When the server arrives, please order a diet for me."

"Where are you going?" Serena asked, alarmed.

"To the bathroom. As long as that's alright with you two?" She eyed them both, then walked away. She stopped a server to ask where the bathroom was, then followed the instructions, turning the corner and waiting a few beats before turning back to the main dining room. As she neared Quentin's booth, she confirmed that the woman with him was Lena. Alex stopped as if she'd just noticed them, then walked directly to their booth. "Mr. Chase, Ms. Foster, what a pleasant surprise."

Quentin looked up, narrowing his eyes, but then he smiled. "It's Quentin, remember? And please call her Lena. What brings you here?"

Alex smiled. "Same thing as you, I imagine. I heard the pizza is phenomenal."

"It definitely is. And why I'm here every day."

"Yes, every single day," Lena said. Alex could tell the woman was less than pleased about it. "Good thing they have decent salads or I'd look like her."

Alex turned to see a healthy looking woman with a few curves threading her way through the tables. She wanted to say something scathing to Lena, but clamped her mouth shut.

"Her?" Quentin asked, while eyeing the woman up and down, evaluating her shapely figure. He returned his focus to Lena, clearly comparing the two and finding her lacking. "Maybe you should eat a pizza now and then."

Alex interrupted before things could get out of hand. She didn't have the time to deal with their obviously dysfunctional relationship, whatever it was. "I'm actually seated in the booth next to you and I couldn't help but overhear your plans to visit Belize. It's a wonderful place, and I'm sure you two will love it."

Quentin frowned, glaring at Lena before responding to Alex. "I'm afraid you're mistaken."

"About?"

"Two things: one, Ms. Foster is my public relations assistant, nothing more. And two, I have neither the time nor the inclination to be jetting off to some backwards country just because it has a beach. We've got plenty of beaches right here and besides, my focus is on the sanctuary for the foreseeable future."

Alex struggled to keep her attention on Quentin, although part of her really wanted to see the expression on Lena's face at both the use of her surname and the denial that the two had any sort of relationship. "My apologies. I'm afraid I fell into the trap of assuming."

"You wouldn't be the only one," Quentin said, glowering at Lena.

Instead of accepting her boss's thinly veiled insults like a good little employee, Lena leaned back, tilting her head and giving him an enigmatic smile before shifting her attention to Alex. "Don't mind Quentin," she said, her voice unexpectedly seductive. "He sometimes forgets what's good for him. When you handle PR for a man like him, you learn where all the bodies are buried."

Aha, Alex thought. She smiled at the other woman. "I'm sure you do. I'll bet you know all his secrets. Say, for example, where he was Tuesday night?"

Quentin opened his mouth, but before he could say anything, Wyatt jumped out of the booth. "What are you doing?" he shouted. "We agreed to work together on this."

Alex clenched her fists, but kept the smile firmly planted on her face. She'd known working with Wyatt would be problematic, but didn't feel she had a choice. She reminded herself that the only way she knew Quentin would be at the restaurant was because of the activist. "Of course, Wyatt. I was surprised to see them on my way back from the ladies' room and thought it would be rude not to say hi."

"Work together on what?" Quentin asked. Wyatt moved back as Serena slid out of the booth. "And I suppose she's working with you, too?"

Alex kept smiling. "As a matter of fact, yes. After the reception the other night– which was fabulous, by the way–the three of us realized we're all on the same page."

"And what page is that?" Quentin asked.

"Probably has something to do with the rising levels of toxic chemicals in our drinking water," Lena drawled, picking up her glass and holding it up to the light. "Hard to believe something that looks so innocuous could kill people." She put her glass back down on the table and looked directly at Quentin. "Although it seems crystal-clear to me what's going on."

"And that is?" Quentin growled. Alex prayed Wyatt and Serena wouldn't interrupt.

"Why, somebody's trying to frame you, of course."

Wyatt burst out laughing. Serena, to her credit, stayed silent, but she did reach for her phone and Alex could see her open a recording app. Alex nodded slightly at the young woman.

"Frame me for what? And how? I swear, Lena, your imagination is getting out of control."

"Better for me to imagine someone is framing you than the alternative, wouldn't you say?"

Quentin stared at her. "Fine. I'll bite. Just what do you think is going on? And who do you think is 'framing' me and for what?" He finally seemed to realize they had an audience and impatiently waved his hand at them. "If you could excuse us; this is none of your business."

Alex pulled a chair from the table behind her and sat down. She crossed her legs, then plucked an invisible piece of lint from her pants. She felt her phone vibrate again, but she ignored it. "Actually, this is exactly the business we wanted to talk to you about. But please, Lena, don't let us interrupt. I'm curious what you think is happening."

Lena appraised her, then gave her a small, almost feral smile. It reminded Alex a bit of Cassidy when the archaeologist was about ready to pounce. "Since I, as Quentin put it, am his public relations assistant, it's my job to anticipate any potential scandals." She focused on her boss. "Did you know, for example, that barrels with Quentum Corp's logo have been found near the S.S. Senator?"

Alex could see the shock on Quentin's face. Wyatt gasped. "How did you–" he asked.

"Like I said. It's my job." Lena turned enough to focus on Serena. "I was working with Ben to find out who's behind the dumping."

Several things from the last few days clicked and Alex knew. "You were his inside source."

Lena nodded with approval. "Yes. We were working together to prove that Quentum Corp and, therefore, Quentin Chase, had and has nothing to do with what's happening to the lake. How profoundly stupid would that be? To make a reputation as someone trying to protect those shipwrecks and to be a primary influence in bringing the sanctuary here, and then to destroy the very things he's trying to save? Quentin Chase may be many things, but stupid is definitely not one of them."

"Thanks for that resounding endorsement," Quentin said wryly.

"I don't buy it," Wyatt said. "This is exactly the thing someone like you would do to try to make it seem like you wouldn't be the one doing it." Alex sighed, both for his convoluted phrasing and his contention. Wyatt glared at her. "It *is* something he'd do, and you know it. He'd be the last person anyone would think would be dumping his crap into the lake, especially not near his precious wreck. But you know what? We've got proof," he spat.

Quentin chuckled, shaking his head. "Do you ever get tired of tilting at windmills?"

"Careful," Lena warned her boss, although her expression said she was enjoying herself. "You may have the local press sewn up, thanks to me, but she," Lena pointed at Serena, "is from one of the biggest newspapers in the country. You should probably be a little nicer."

"I wasn't speaking to her," Quentin said. "I was speaking to him. And I'm done." He reached his arm out and snapped his fingers at a passing server. "We're done here. Add whatever they get to my tab."

Wyatt began to thank him, but Serena cut him off. "No thank you. Ethically, I can't accept that. We'll pay our own bills."

"Speak for yourself," Wyatt muttered.

"Fine." Quentin scooted towards the end of the booth and Alex moved out of his way. He pushed through Serena and Wyatt, leaving Lena behind, then stopped at the entrance to the restaurant. He turned, practically tapping his foot with impatience. Lena leisurely extracted herself from the seat, then turned to Alex, her back to Quentin. She pulled out a card and handed it to her.

"Give me ten minutes, then call me. Plan to meet me at five. I'll tell you where"

Alex narrowed her eyes. "Why?"

"Ben told me about you. Said I could trust you." Lena swept her eyes over Wyatt and Serena. "But only you. He died for this, so don't prove him a liar."

"Died for what? Lena, what's happening? Is Quentin behind all this?"

Lena didn't answer. "Ten minutes," she said, then turned around and walked towards her boss.

Wyatt expelled a hot breath. "Well, that was interesting. Should we order something while we wait until you can call? I know *you're* too goody goody to be on his tab," he said to Serena, "but I'm hungry."

Serena glared at him as he sat down in their original booth and looked over the menu. "What do you think she's going to tell you?" she asked Alex.

"I have no idea," Alex answered, even though that wasn't quite true. She had a very good idea what Lena wanted to tell her. At least, she hoped she did.

Chapter 20

Alex pulled her phone out to turn the ringer back on. There was a call from an unknown number, but no voice mail, and a couple of texts from Ethan. She didn't want to open them, not sure she could handle any more disappointment, but she still needed his help.

I'm sorry. I know it's not my place to tell you what to do. I'm just concerned because I care about you.

Alex sighed. She felt a jumble of emotions, none of which she could deal with at the moment. She scrolled up to read his last message.

I just saw Quentin leave. He looked angry. You OK?

At that, Alex smiled. Good. That meant Ethan was outside. It also meant he'd been following her and Wyatt. She'd deal with that another time. She started to leave, then remembered something. "When we first got here, you heard them say something that surprised you."

"We did?" Serena asked. "Oh, yeah. That's right. Lena was ticked because Quentin kicked her out Tuesday night."

"'Ticked' is an understatement. Sounded like this wasn't the first time they'd fought about it." Wyatt laughed, clearly thrilled by their discontent.

"Wait a minute," Alex said to Serena. "I thought you said you overheard them at the reception, and that she was with him. That's what gave Quentin an alibi."

"Turns out, he didn't want her to stay all night in case somebody saw her leaving in the morning," Serena said smugly. "Probably didn't want anyone to think he's sleeping with the help."

"Which is exactly what Lena said. Wow, was she mad."

Alex understood. She'd be angry, too. "You know what that means…"

Serena grinned. "Yep. No more alibi."

"Who cares about the alibi?" Wyatt grunted. "I'm more interested in what she had to say about the sanctuary."

"Which was?" Alex prompted.

"That she knew all he cared about were those stupid Nash autos, that the shipwrecks meant nothing to him besides adding to his collection and he better be careful how he talked to her. Talk about a woman scorned."

Alex thought about the implications. She hesitated just a moment, but she knew what she needed to do, and it didn't involve these two. She looked at her phone and acted like she was reading a message. "I've got to go," she said.

"What? You can't leave, not without us," Wyatt protested.

Serena's eyes narrowed. "You're planning on keeping us out of the loop?"

"Something's come up. That's all. I'll talk to you both later."

Wyatt scrambled out of the booth. "Wait just a minute. I know what you're up to. You're going to screw us over, aren't you? Typical. I knew all you cared about was finding out who killed your stupid ex-boyfriend."

"Don't you see they're related?" Alex huffed. "Whoever is polluting the lake–"

"Which is obviously Quentin Chase."

"–is the same person who killed Ben. It's the only thing that makes sense."

"But Lena seems to think someone's trying to frame Quentin for the murder," Serena said, "so that means it was somebody else. Who'd want to frame him?"

Wyatt guffawed. "Some reporter you are. He's got more enemies than I do."

"And since it seems you get some perverse joy out of making people angry, that's saying something," Serena muttered.

Alex checked her watch. Four minutes had already passed. "I said I'll talk to you later. Now I really have to go." She turned and walked towards the door without looking back, slightly surprised they didn't follow her, but figured they were probably shocked she'd actually left. She exited the restaurant and looked to the right, then to the left, where she saw Ethan's car. She quickly walked towards him. When he made a move to get out of the vehicle, she shook her head and sped up, reaching the door in seconds and hopping in. Wyatt and Serena burst out of the restaurant, and just like she had, looked to the right first. Alex scooted down in her seat. "Would you please very quickly do a u-turn and head the other direction? Oh, and don't look towards the restaurant, if you wouldn't mind." She kept her head down, hoping the other two wouldn't recognize Ethan's car or see him behind the wheel.

Ethan looked down at her, but followed her directions. "I must say, for someone who's on the lam, you seem to be very calm."

"First of all, I am not on the lam. I'm merely trying to avoid dealing with two people who are, quite frankly, getting in my way."

She sat up slightly, just enough to see out the window and determine that Wyatt and Serena were still looking around and not paying attention to Ethan's car. "Besides, if I came in here acting panicked and shouting at you to move the blooming vehicle, you'd pull out your lawyer voice and ask me what was wrong and before we knew it, those two would've been pounding on the window."

Ethan chuckled. "Fair enough. Now, speaking of fair, care to tell me what's going on?"

Alex checked her watch. It was time. She pulled out Lena's card and dialed the number. "Later," she said to Ethan with barely enough time to get the word out before Lena answered.

"Right on time. Thank you, because I don't have much to spare. I'll cut right to the chase, so to speak," Lena said, then chuckled at her own pun. "Quentin couldn't have murdered Ben."

"How do you know that?" Alex didn't want to tell Lena she knew she couldn't provide Quentin's alibi. Mentioning that would be sure to get her defenses up.

"Because I was with him Tuesday night."

"All night?"

Lena sighed. "Fine. No. Not all night. I left around ten."

"Then how do you know he couldn't have murdered him?"

"Because I followed him, alright? He asked me to leave with some lame excuse about keeping things between us quiet. Not that anything had actually happened. I was furious. I waited outside, sure he was going to meet someone."

"And was he?"

"Yes." Lena paused.

"Who did he meet, Lena?" Alex asked softly.

"Ben."

Alex gripped her phone, forcing herself to remain calm.

"I know, I know," Lena said. "But it's not what you think. He got to the marina and they walked out together on the breakwater. Towards the lighthouse."

"This isn't sounding good. You know that's where I found Ben." Alex waited, noticing Ethan was slowing down. He pulled into a parking lot next to a beach and stopped, facing the lake. A surfer swam towards the waves, his black wetsuit shining, beads of water sparkling in the afternoon sun. Ethan reached over to take her free hand and squeezed lightly.

"Yes, of course I know," Lena said, her voice strident. "Would you let me finish? They walked out together, and then walked back. Before Quentin left, they shook hands, and I could have sworn he passed something to Ben."

"Why?"

"Because Quentin doesn't shake hands. The only time he'll touch anyone is if he wants something or needs to exert his dominance."

This didn't make sense to Alex. Why was Lena telling her all this? And why would she put herself in a position to be treated like that by a man? *Stop*, Alex chided herself. *It's not your place to judge*.

"What happened then?"

"Quentin left."

"Did you follow him?"

"No. I–I got out and talked to Ben." Lena paused. "I know this looks bad, but when I left, he was still alive."

"Why? Why did you talk to him?"

"Because I loved him," Lena spat. "Happy now?"

Alex stared at the phone in shock. That was the last thing she'd expected to hear. Serena was smitten with her ex, and now Lena was, too, and yet Ben had been stalking Alex and was under the delusion that she'd go back to him. But, she reminded herself of the beginning of their relationship, when his charm swept her off her feet, when she'd been besotted with him. It took cancer for her to see his manipulations. Which made her wonder: what had he wanted from Lena?

"I'm so sorry, Lena. I didn't know. Do you mind if I ask how long you've known him?"

"Yes, I mind. What—you think because we'd only met a few weeks ago it wasn't love? You knew him. You dated him. From what I heard, you were in love with him until he dumped you. Seems to me you'd have the biggest motive."

Alex stared at the phone, incredulous, but she kept her tone sympathetic. "Yes, Ben definitely knew how to inspire strong emotions. But I didn't kill him, and I don't think you believe I did, or you wouldn't be telling me all of this."

Lena grunted. "I know you didn't. Cassidy told me you were on their boat all night."

"How in the.. Why would she tell you that?"

"Should be obvious. Because they've been working with Dr. Moore to catalog details on the shipwrecks."

"And you've been helping the sanctuary with their press."

"Exactly. We were prepping for the gala when we heard about Ben's death. I immediately accused you of killing him and Cassidy said that was impossible."

Alex breathed a sigh of relief. Now, if only Detective Stephens would believe Cassidy as much as Lena did, but the police officer seemed to think Alex could have snuck out in the middle of the night.

"Yes?" Lena said, her voice muffled. "Be right there." She spoke again, this time her voice clearer. "I have to go."

"Wait. Where am I supposed to meet you?"

"Write this down." Lena gave her an address. Alex grabbed her pen and notebook from her bag, grateful she always had them handy. "Five p.m. Don't be late. I won't have much time."

She hung up and Alex stared through the windshield, barely registering the surfer as he navigated the waves before falling into the frigid water. What Lena said made no sense. It seemed she was having an affair with Quentin, but also said she loved Ben. Could she have been playing Quentin? Or, like Serena, were her feelings for Ben unrequited? It was amazing how much upheaval one man could cause.

Alex shivered, both in sympathy and with apprehension. Ethan cleared his throat.

"Everything alright?"

"Maybe. Lena wants me to meet her at at five. Could you take me? I'm sorry to keep imposing on you like to this, to involve you."

"I know you'd rather have William helping you."

"Of course I would. No offense, but we've been through a lot together. And besides, I don't want any of this to cause you any problems."

"You've already caused me lots of problems, Alex Paige."

Alex tore her eyes from the horizon and turned to face Ethan. He was looking at her in a way that made her feel warm inside, but also made her want to instinctively pull back. *He really is a good man.* Maybe later, when this was over, they'd be able to see if there was something between them. She put her hand on his cheek, smiling at him tenderly. "I've always said I should come with a warning label."

Ethan laughed, breaking the spell. "That you definitely should. Now, what's next?"

Alex smiled, then reached in the back for Ben's laptop bag. "Lena said she saw Quentin give Ben something. I'm assuming it was a flash drive. I must have missed it earlier because I was so focused on his computer." She rummaged through the pockets, then felt something at the bottom of one of them. "There we go. Now let's see what's on this bad boy."

Chapter 21

Ethan drove the winding road, keeping his speed to just above the limit. While Alex generally liked to drive no more than five miles over, his caution annoyed her. She knew it was because she had to rely on him to drive her everywhere, and that made her both irritable and increasingly impatient. She checked her watch for at least the tenth time since they'd left the coffee shop where she'd been holed up for the last few hours. After hanging up with Lena, Alex had insisted he drop her off and then pick her up later so she could review the contents of the USB drive in private. Ethan had resisted, but finally gave in and left her on her own.

What she'd seen was definitely not what she'd expected. It shocked her, but it was obvious why Quentin had given Ben the information on the drive, and equally obvious what he'd hoped to get out of it. Well, she had a suspicion about what the CEO hoped to gain, and hopefully Lena would be able to prove whether she was correct, or incorrect. As the woman had said, she knew where the bodies were buried.

Alex glanced at the speedometer again, willing Ethan to move it a little faster. They were cutting it close, and she knew this was her last chance to find out what happened. William and Billy's rehearsal dinner was in two and a half hours, and Alex was determined to be there.

"Should I drop you at the entrance?" Ethan asked.

"Please."

"Want me to come with you?"

"No," Alex snapped, then took a breath. "Thank you. I'm afraid if you're there, Lena will clam up. She said to come alone."

Ethan nodded. "I'll be right there," he said, pointing to an empty parking spot as he slowed down.

Alex opened the door and started to get out, then leaned back in and kissed him on the cheek. "Thank you," she said again, this time whispering in his ear. "I owe you."

"Yes, you do," he said, winking. "Now go. Find out what Lena has to say. Oh—and I do expect a full debriefing once you've got this all figured out, including what was on that drive."

"Got it," Alex said, stepping out of the vehicle and closing the door behind her. She passed under a bronze arch sculpted with fanciful whorls into a garden themed around children's books. Her phone buzzed. It was a text from Lena.

Ticket at counter. Meet at Horton.

Alex frowned, but she walked to the ticket counter and gave her name. A young woman handed her a ticket. "Could you tell me where Horton is?" Alex asked.

"Oh, that's one of my favorites! Just follow that path around. You can't miss him. He's an elephant in a tree, after all."

Alex followed the directions, picking up a path that skirted the outside of the gardens. She wished she had time to stroll. Many of her favorite stories from her childhood—Frog and Toad, {add more here}--were represented in this charming place. They'd even laminated the books so children could take the stories with them as they explored. Because it was October, the gardens were decorated for Halloween, with bushes wearing googly eyes and trees strung with spider webs.

She saw the red egg with white polka dots first, then spied Horton's trunk. Next to the tree, Lena stood with Dr. Moore. Alex paused for just a moment, then continued walking towards the women. "This is a surprise," Alex said warily. Although she'd gotten a good impression of the sanctuary's director at the gala, she thought of what she'd seen earlier that afternoon and put her guard up. Alex hated the necessity of constant vigilance, and it was one of the reasons she'd left investigative reporting. She pasted a smile on her face and extended her hand. "Good to see you, Celeste."

"Sorry to surprise you like this, but Lena convinced me to talk to you."

Alex studied her. She thought again about the files Quentin had given to Ben, and spoke to Lena. "I know we don't have much time. Did you talk to Ben that night? After Quentin left the marina?"

"Briefly."

"What did he say?"

"Nothing. Nothing of substance, anyway. Said Quentin had promised him proof of who was dumping, but that was it. He wouldn't tell me any more. He told me to stay out of it, for my own good."

Alex laughed. "Something I'd heard from him multiple times." She turned to Celeste. "I'm assuming you know everything?"

The doctor sighed. "Not everything, no. I know somebody's been polluting the lake. I know somebody's been looting the shipwrecks. I know Quentin claims he has nothing to do with either. And I know your friend died because of this. But that's all I know."

"Celeste, we know who's polluting the lake," Lena said.

"You do?" Alex asked.

"We have no proof," Celeste said through clenched teeth. "Not any more."

"Is that why you wanted me to meet you?"

"Yes, because without proof, we're too close to Quentin for anyone to take us seriously. I've planted the idea that I was having an affair with him, so nobody's going to believe me—that whole woman scorned thing—and Celeste owes her job at the sanctuary to him."

Celeste visibly bristled. "I have earned my position."

Lena rolled her eyes. "Yes, you have, but Quentin made it easier."

"Whose side are you on?"

"Mine," Lena said. "And yours, because I know you have nothing to do with what's happening."

"Are you sure about that?" Alex asked.

Both women snapped their heads towards her. "What do you mean? Of course I didn't. This is the polar opposite of what I stand for," Celeste protested.

Alex believed her, despite what she'd seen in the files Quentin had given to Ben. First, though, she needed to clear something up. "Lena, what do you mean you planted the idea you were having an affair with him?"

"Exactly that. I created an illusion."

"Why?"

"Because then I could do what I needed to do to find out what was happening. If his lackeys thought I had a, quote-unquote, special relationship with him, they'd be less likely to question me when, say, they saw me in his office when he wasn't around."

"But why? Why would you go through all that?"

"Because I loathe Quentin Chase and everything he stands for," Lena snapped. "He's a misogynistic narcissist who destroys everything and everyone who's in his way. He's pure evil. If it weren't for him, Ben would still be alive. If it weren't for him..." she stopped, her eyes filling with tears. She turned away, and both Alex and Celeste gave her a moment to compose herself. Lena cleared her throat, then turned back. "If it weren't for him, my parents would still be alive," she said, her voice clear and strong.

Celeste reached out as if to rub her back, but stopped herself before touching the austere woman. Alex waited. "Cancer," Celeste explained. "They retired to a beautiful town on a beautiful lake north of here. They loved hiking and fishing and kayaking. They were fit. They were healthy.

"And then they moved to this supposedly idyllic place and six years later they were dead. Bladder cancer. Want to know where they lived?"

"Clearwater Hills?" Alex guessed.

"Yes," Lena said. Her voice broke, but she cleared her throat to cover it up. "Quentin built his first factory a few miles upstream from the town. Nobody knew what was going on, that he was literally pumping his waste into the lake, until more and more people got sick. By the time anyone decided to do something about it, he'd already closed down and moved down here. Got slapped with a fine and that was it."

This time Celeste reached out and did touch Lena, trying to offer her comfort. Lena shrugged it off. She focused on Alex, the anger emanating from her eyes. "I spent the next ten years worming my way in, making myself indispensable. But I had no idea what to do. And then I met Celeste. I hated her," she said, giving the doctor a small smile.

Celeste laughed. "The feeling was mutual, I'm afraid. But we quickly learned we had a common enemy."

"Quentin?" Alex guessed. "But you were his head of R&D."

"Exactly. I'd heard about what happened in Clearwater Hills, of course, but I knew if I were on the inside, I could make sure everything was disposed of properly. And then he hired Martin, and Quentin got involved with the sanctuary."

"Who's Martin?" Alex asked, confused.

"My 'replacement.' Supposedly a genius when it comes to nanocoating, but more like a genius in brown nosing and taking shortcuts, the very shortcuts that got Quentin in trouble the first time. But I didn't know, and when he suggested me for the position as director of the sanctuary, I leapt at it," Celeste said, then spoke softly to Lena. "I thought Martin would make sure the protocols I'd put in place would stay."

"That sniveling sycophant?" Lena sneered. "You know better than that. He'd literally lick Quentin's boots if he asked him. That's why I did what I had to do."

Her statement confused Alex, but just for a moment. "By getting close to him?"

"Yes. I had to act like he could do no wrong. I had to act like I was smitten with him. I had to throw myself at him. It was the only way I could think of to find the proof I needed to make him pay for Mom and Dad."

Knowing that Lena had willingly put herself close to the man responsible for her parents' death horrified Alex. "Did you know about her parents?" she asked Celeste.

She shook her head. "Not at first. It took awhile for us to trust each other. We were both there undercover, so to speak. I worked for him because his product is revolutionary, but somebody needed to mitigate the damage he could do. I knew I had to show him how he could actually save money by doing the right thing."

Alex narrowed her eyes. "And the sanctuary? Whose idea was it to create that?"

Celeste grunted. "Not mine. Not Quentin's either. This has been in the works for years."

"I know that," Alex stopped her, waving her hand impatiently. "I meant, whose idea was it to get Quentin involved in it."

Lena smiled slyly. "That was my doing. Quentin took a hit once Wyatt and his group started publicizing the stories of Clearwater Hills again, and I still didn't have the proof I needed. So, I told him the best way to counteract all that negative publicity would be to appear as a staunch environmentalist, someone who would pony up his own money to protect the lake."

"*Appear* being the operative word," Celeste said. "Quentin Chase doesn't care one iota if what he does kills people."

"So what do you think is happening?" Alex asked.

"It's not what we think; it's what we know," Lena said. "Celeste caught him. She caught him red-handed."

"What do you mean?"

Celeste opened her mouth to speak, but stopped as a family approached. A young boy held a copy of *Horton Hears a Who!*, and his mom squatted next to him and began reading from the book while the toddler turned the laminated pages. Lena walked away; Celeste and Alex followed. The three women neared an arched bridge over a narrow creek and stopped in the middle. They leaned on the railing. Celeste and Alex flanked Lena, and

Celeste resumed speaking, her voice hushed. "I went out on the water with Tom Harris. He's been acting as a consultant for the sanctuary."

Alex nodded. "I've met him. He's friends with Cassidy and Reid."

"The archaeologists. Right. Anyway, Tom had gotten a report that there's been some suspicious late night activity at the marina." Celeste swallowed. When she spoke again, her voice was filled with anger. "He got a tip from one of his buddies that there seemed to be a pattern; once a week, a small barge would head out after midnight. On Monday night, we followed it."

That explained the cryptic emails between Ben and Tom, Alex realized.

"And there he was," Celeste continued. "Quentin Chase himself directing his lackeys to dump a whole pallet of barrels into the lake. And we got it all on video."

Chapter 22

Celeste should have sounded triumphant. Instead, she sounded defeated. "What happened?" Alex asked, even though she had a pretty good idea.

"Quentin found out." Celeste swallowed. "I was so *stupid*," she berated herself.

"Stop it," Lena said, the force of her voice surprising Alex. "Stop beating yourself up."

Celeste stood up, clenching her fists. "Why shouldn't I? I should have known better than to use my work phone."

"You didn't do it on purpose, remember? We've been over this. You simply grabbed the wrong one." Lena's voice was surprisingly soothing.

Alex had a pretty clear picture of what happened. "Let me guess: you've got a personal phone, and another one you use for the sanctuary." When Celeste nodded, Alex continued. "You shot the video on that one."

"Yes," Celeste spat. "Completely forgetting that Quentin provided the cell phones for the sanctuary, one of his magnanimous gestures. And guess what? All photos and videos are automatically backed up to the cloud. As soon as I got back home and my phone connected to my wifi, all that proof was uploaded."

"And he could see all of it."

"And then he deleted it. Deleting it from the cloud also removes it from my phone. It's gone. It's completely gone." Celeste slumped. "And worse, he knows I did it."

"I'm afraid it's even worse than that," Alex said. Both Lena and Celeste stared at her.

"How could it be worse?" Lena asked.

"He's trying to pin it on you." Alex looked around. "This is what he gave to Ben that night." Alex pulled out her phone and opened the gallery. "I found the USB drive Quentin had given to Ben in his laptop bag–don't ask why I have that– in one of the pockets. This was on it."

Alex hit play, and the screen filled with grainy footage. A barge rocked gently on the water. Figures moved in and out of the frame, silhouetted against the reflection of the moon on the lake's surface. Two men hoisted a pallet of barrels toward the edge of the barge, while a third figure stood nearby, gesturing sharply.

The camera panned and zoomed slightly, focusing on the person directing the operation.

Celeste gasped. "That isn't me," she protested.

"Her" face was illuminated as she barked orders. The voice was distorted but just clear enough to resemble the doctor's tone.

The two men in the video tipped the barrels into the water, one by one, the sound of splashes muffled under the din of machinery and waves lapping at the boat. The figure glanced up, towards the camera, and the resemblance was uncanny. For anyone watching, there would be no doubt who it was.

Alex heard conversation, and she turned to see a large gaggle of children. A cluster of parents trailed them and they approached the bridge. She paused the video and smiled briefly at the boisterous group before leaning back over the railing.

"How do you know that isn't me?" Celeste asked, her voice shaky.

"The height. You're taller than Quentin."

"They even got my voice," Celeste said, shaking her head. "Quentin doesn't know how to do this."

"But Martin does," Lena said.

"Yes, yes I do."

Alex spun. Martin stood within inches, his face pale but his expression set. He seemed defiant, or maybe that was just because he was pointing a small gun. Although it was partially obscured by his jacket, Alex could clearly see it, along with his trembling hand.

The group of kids and parents continued to cross the bridge, oblivious to what was happening. Alex shifted slightly, positioning herself between Martin and the children without drawing attention to the weapon.

"Martin," she said evenly, forcing herself to focus on his eyes and ignore the gun. "You don't have to do this."

"Don't I?" His voice cracked. "You don't understand. I don't have a choice."

"What, because you're afraid of big bad Quentin?" Lena interjected, her voice scathing. "Grow a spine."

Alex glared at her. Was she trying to get them killed? "Look, Martin," Alex said. "I know you feel like you're protecting yourself, but this is only going to make things worse." She hoped by speaking calmly, she'd be able to deescalate the situation. "You know the truth is going to come out."

Martin shook his head violently. "The truth? The truth doesn't matter," he scoffed. "Perception does. If people think Celeste did this, Quentin's safe, Quentum Corp is safe, and everything stays the way it is. That's what matters." He gestured to Alex's phone with the barrel of the gun. "People believe what they see with their own eyes, and that video is all they'll ever see."

Alex's grip tightened around her phone. "Why, Martin? Why are you doing this?"

"Yes, Martin. Do tell. Why are you doing Quentin's dirty work? Isn't it enough he treats you like a puppy dog?" Lena sneered.

Martin's lips twitched and he stepped closer to her, jabbing the gun in her stomach. "Go ahead. Laugh. But it takes one to know one, doesn't it? You and your '*Yes, Mr. Chase. Of course, Mr. Chase. Should I take my clothes off for you, Mr. Chase?*' Disgusting," he spat.

Lena laughed. *What was she doing?* Alex wondered. She was going to get them all killed.

Celeste took a step forward, her fists clenched. "You're a coward," she spat. "At least Lena knows what's right and wrong. You're just a puppet."

Martin's face flushed, and his grip on the gun wavered. "I'm not a puppet! Without me, Quentin would be nothing!"

Alex caught movement out of the corner of her eye and realized why Lena and Celeste were being so confrontational. She didn't agree with it, but she understood it. "Then why are you the one standing here, covering for him?" Alex shot back, joining in. "Why are you risking everything while he's safe, probably sipping scotch while you do all the dirty work?"

Martin flinched, the crack in his composure widening. For a moment, his eyes darted to the children, who were gathered around a firepit, far enough away they couldn't hear anything. One of the parents distributed marshmallows on metal pokers and another made sure the kids stayed a safe distance from the flames. The sight seemed to unnerve him, and his hand shook visibly.

"You don't understand," he muttered, his voice barely audible. "I don't have a choice," he repeated.

"You always have a choice," Lena said, stepping closer. Her tone was gentle now, soothing. "But if you keep going down this path, the choice will be taken away from you. Quentin won't protect you. That's not who he is."

Martin's mouth opened, but no words came out. The seconds stretched, the only sound the murmurs of the group at the other end of the bridge.

Alex seized the moment. "Put the gun down, Martin," she said softly. "Let's end this. No one has to get hurt."

Martin hesitated. He lowered the gun ever so slightly. But just as Alex thought she might have reached him, a high-pitched voice called from beyond the far end of the bridge.

"Daddy, look! It's Goldilocks!"

Martin's head snapped up at the sound of the child's voice, his grip tightening on the gun. His eyes darted toward the family group clustered around the fire, and for one terrifying second, Alex thought he might do something reckless. Instead, he took a step back, his face crumpling with anguish. *Just a few more moments*, Alex thought.

"I didn't want this," he whispered, before turning and bolting toward the opposite end of the bridge.

And smack dab into Detective Stephens and Officer Rourke. Rourke plucked the gun from Martin's hand and passed it to another police officer before spinning him around and clinching handcuffs around his wrists.

"Martin Lang, we need to you to come with us."

Chapter 23

The skin of the bratwurst snapped as Alex bit into it. She wiped brown mustard from the corner of her mouth and licked her finger. "Only you would have brats and potato salad catered for your rehearsal dinner."

"When in Sheboygan!" William grinned. "You can't come to Sheboygan and not have a brat."

"It is the brat capital of the world, after all," Billy said.

"Hmm. Brat capital of the world. Freshwater surfing capital of the world. Who knew?" Ethan asked.

"We did!" Juke and Evie chorused. Considering they lived just a couple of hours away, it made sense they'd know.

The friends laughed. They had all gathered in William's and Billy's suite. It wasn't your typical rehearsal dinner. As William had told Alex, it was basically an excuse for them to all get together before the big day.

The door opened and Cassidy and Reid swept in. "Sorry we're late," she said before draping her coat over the back of the couch and joining them in the dining area.

"Detective Stephens had a few more questions for us about what the ROV found," Reid explained.

"Alex was just starting to tell us what happened. I still can't believe you kept me out of everything," William pouted.

"It all turned out fine," she said.

"Sure. Fine. Only you had a gun pointed at you—again. Seriously. I can't leave you alone for a minute," he complained. "And you even promised me no dead bodies." Alex blinked and he immediately looked abashed. "I'm sorry. That was awful."

Alex nodded. The comment subdued the celebration.

"I really am sorry, Alex."

"I know," she said, then gave him a tender smile. "It's okay. Really. The whole thing is just sad."

"So did Martin kill Ben, then?" Billy asked.

Alex looked at Ethan. The two had arrived at the couple's nontraditional rehearsal dinner right on time, despite having to go to the police station with Lena and Celeste, but they hadn't explained anything yet. "No," he said.

Everyone looked at Ethan, then at Alex, then back at Ethan.

"Well then, who did?" Evie asked.

"Nobody," Alex said.

"What?" It was a collective exclamation.

"Nobody," she repeated. "Nobody killed Ben. It was a stupid accident." She got up and stood at the window, gazing in the distance to the breakwater.

Ethan explained. "Turns out he'd had a couple cocktails before we saw him at the restaurant. Then several more after he met with Quentin and talked to Lena. The yacht club kicked him out at closing; the bartender said he kept saying he'd find her, she couldn't be far, he knew where she'd be in the morning and he'd just wait for her."

"Her, meaning Alex, I'm assuming?" Cassidy asked softly.

Ethan nodded. "Remember how cold it was that night?"

Reid nodded. "Freezing. I'd forgotten some water out on the deck and when we got back to the boat, there was ice on top."

"And it only got colder. Plus, that wind created some pretty big waves."

"Which crashed on the breakwater. I had to be careful when I walked out to the lighthouse that morning to avoid slipping on the ice," Alex said, still looking out the window. She turned around and rejoined them at the dining room table.

"So Ben fell and hit his head?" Billy asked.

Alex nodded. "Yes. When I was sound asleep, he was out there dying."

William sprang up and walked over to her. He grabbed her hands and waited until she met his eyes. "Alex Paige, it is not your fault he died. He died because he was stalking you."

"That doesn't mean he deserved it."

"That is not what I said. But what I am saying is that you had nothing to do with it, and I hereby forbid you to blame yourself. Got it?" He gave her his sternest expression and refused to relent until she nodded slightly. "Good. Now, how did you find all this out?"

Alex waited until he released her hands and returned to his place next to Billy. "I called Ophelia—Detective Stephens—this afternoon. I decided you were right," she said to Ethan, "and that I couldn't keep running. So, I told her I knew she probably had a warrant for my arrest, and then I let her know what time I'd be at the gardens. She stopped me before I could finish and told me they'd gotten the autopsy results. Both the toxicology report and the nature of his injury told them his death had been accidental."

Ethan shook his head. "I still can't believe you didn't tell me."

"She does that," William said. "Keeps things all mysterious. Drives me batty."

"Sometimes I'm wrong. And I didn't want to worry you," she said to Ethan.

"Here's what I don't get," Juke said. It was the first thing he'd said since Alex and Ethan had gotten there, besides hugging her and telling her he was glad she wasn't a murderer. "Why'd you still meet Lena?"

"Because I'd seen the video of Celeste. I knew it had to be a fake. I couldn't just ignore it."

"So what happens now?" Juke asked.

"What happens now," Alex said, picking up her glass and raising her arm, "is we celebrate the love of these two incredible people. William and Billy, congratulations, and I can't wait to see you tie the knot tomorrow."

"Cheers to that!" William said, grabbing his fiancé and holding him tightly.

The door opened, interrupting the tender moment. "Hey hey everybody. Now the party can start!"

William released Billy and ran towards the door. A woman with fuschia hair waited, her arms outstretched. "Emily!"

Alex grinned. Her two best friends had met a year ago and had hit it off famously. She got up and crossed the room also, albeit a bit more sedately than William had. She hugged Emily, who squeezed her tightly and then pulled back to study her.

"I'm so sorry."

Alex gave her a sad smile. "Thank you. I know you didn't like him."

"What was there to like? And what's this I hear about you punching him? Awesome." Emily held her hand up for a high-five.

Alex gave her a baleful look and ignored it. "Right. Sorry. So since you're not in handcuffs, I'm assuming they found out who killed him?"

"Nobody did," William said. "Can you believe it? It was an accident."

"Couldn't have happened to a nicer…" Emily noticed the look on Alex's face and stopped herself. "Sorry. Again. What say we change the subject, because you've had a rough week and I'm making it worse." She took William's arm, and looked towards Billy. "And there's the lucky guy."

"I sure am," Billy said with a smile.

She crossed the room to give him a hug, then William introduced her to Cassidy, Reid, Juke, and Evie. She'd already met Ethan when they were in North Carolina that summer. "Thanks for letting me crash your get-together," she said. "I know I'm not part of the wedding party, and I appreciate getting a chance to see you before all your friends and loved ones descend."

The fiancés grinned at each other, and Billy spoke. "Didn't William tell you? It's just us."

They all looked at them with surprise. "What? But William loves parties," Ethan said. "I've only spent a little time with him, but even I know that."

"Oh, it's still going to be a party, but this way, we can spend time with people we love."

Emily blushed. "Well then, I'm truly honored."

"You should be," William winked.

"Don't let him fool you, though," Billy said. "We're having a huge shindig when we get back home."

"You said shindig," William giggled.

"Careful," Juke said. "Before you know it, you'll be traipsing around the country in his campervan living like a hippie."

Evie eyed him. "Traipsing? Really?"

Juke shrugged. "Apparently I've spent too much time with him this week. Better watch that or I'll be traipsing myself."

Everyone laughed. Emily helped herself to a brat and some potato salad, and they all scooted to make room for her. Alex looked around the table, at this collection of friends she'd made from all over the country. They were so very different, but they had a few things in common. One was that they were, at heart, good people. Another was that they were all passionate about what they'd chosen to do for a living. To them, their livelihoods were avocations, not just jobs. And the third was that they all loved William and, she had no doubt, would love Billy. Juke and Evie already did, as did Alex, and as soon as the rest got to know him, they would, too.

She looked last at Ethan. His head was already turned to her, and she knew he'd been watching her. Alex still didn't know what would happen between them, but decided maybe, just maybe, she'd like to find out.

Epilogue

A slight breeze teased strands of Alex's hair. The sun warmed her skin, but what warmed her from the inside was the two men standing a few feet from her. William and Billy faced each other, grasping hands and grinning like a surfer who'd just caught the perfect wave. There wasn't enough wind for that today, but there was just enough to entice the few sailboats out on the lake. The view made her smile even more as she thought about William's upcoming gift for Billy. He'd continued his lessons that week, without Billy's knowledge, and tomorrow would surprise him by sailing Juke's boat home. Juke would be with them to make sure everything went smoothly, and Evie would drive Billy's car.

Alex shifted her weight. While the gathering was small, she and Juke still stood by their respective groomsmen. They were all resplendent in tuxedos, but William's had a bit more flair, and his sequined lapels sparkled. As they exchanged vows, she wiped a tear and resolutely refused to look at Ethan. While she was definitely interested in a romantic relationship with the attorney, she certainly didn't want to jump head first, and making googly eyes at a wedding was one sure way to send the wrong signal.

Evie stood under the arch strewn with asters. That was another surprise the two men had sprung on them, everyone but Evie, that is. As the owner of an inn in a tourist destination, she'd gotten ordained to act as a backup if someone's chosen officiant was unavailable. They'd asked her as soon as Billy'd said yes, but requested she keep it secret. Alex shook her head again at the two of them, and how they both seemed to delight in surprising people. "We love seeing unexpected joy," William had explained.

Joy was definitely in the air, Alex thought, as she gazed at her friends. Every single one of them, including Ethan, had huge grins on their faces. Especially when Evie said the words they'd all waited to hear:

"I now pronounce you husband and husband!"

Alex opened her laptop and logged into her account with Chicago Standard. There, front and center, was the article she'd been waiting for:

Toxic Secrets Unearthed: Quentin Chase's Crimes Against Lake Michigan and Maritime History

By Serena Dalton

Chicago, IL – The illusion of corporate responsibility shattered this week as Quentin Chase, CEO of Quentum Corp, was arrested for orchestrating the illegal dumping of toxic waste into Lake Michigan and the theft of priceless artifacts from protected ship-wrecks. Chase, once lauded as a pioneer in advanced materials technology, now faces charges that reveal a disturbing legacy of environmental destruction and cultural plunder.

Good job, Serena. The day after the wedding, Alex had invited the young woman to brunch and told her everything she knew. Serena protested, saying Alex should submit it because she'd done all the work.

Alex smiled at her. "Oh no. I left that life for a reason."

"But I thought you wanted back in? Max told me he hired you for the story."

"All I wanted was to find out how Ben died. I did. Serena, you deserve this. You took a chance and came up here all on your own because this is a story you believe in."

Serena swallowed, then grinned. "I won't let you down."

"I know," Alex had said. "I know."

She finished reading the article, closed the laptop, and set it on the table next to her. It was a bit chilly to be sitting on her balcony, but when she'd moved into her condo overlooking Lake Michigan, she'd vowed to take advantage of the view any chance she could. There were still boats out on the water, and it made her think of Billy and William. The two decided to take a slightly delayed honeymoon and were currently testing William's newfound skills in the Caribbean. "Next thing you know, he'll be convincing me to take up scuba diving," William had complained, aghast.

"It would be a good idea if we're going to be sailing more," Billy said.

"I prefer my limited oxygen to come from elevation, not depths." The two had laughed, but Alex had no doubt William was signing up for lessons, if he hadn't already.

She thought, also, of Ethan. He'd be coming out to see her in a few weeks. It would be a get-to-know you visit, and she found herself looking forward to it more than she thought she would.

It felt odd, knowing Ben was no longer around. She hadn't realized how much of a shadow he'd been in her life. While she was sad he'd died, there was an immense feeling of freedom knowing she didn't have to look over her shoulder any more.

Alex felt a warm body rub against her calf and bent down to pick up Ernie. The six-toed cat had hated Ben from the start.

"I wonder what you'll think of Ethan," she said. Ernie purred.

Thank you for spending your time with Alex and friends! For even more Alex, find out how her travel writing career began—with a crime, of course! She's barely off the plane for her first research trip when she encounters the police. Will the Sonoran Desert, and her new career, prove too hot for her to handle? Visit thelocaltourist.com/go/stolen/ to get your free short story, *Stolen on the Salt River*.

BONUS: Save 20% on all Alex Paige mysteries at theresasbooks.com. Use code MENACE20.

Recipe
Oat Fashioned, Courtesy of Black Pig

If the cocktail Alex, Cassidy, Reid, William, and Billy enjoyed at dinner the night they ran into Ben made you thirsty, you're in for a treat. The Oat Fashioned is a signature cocktail at Black Pig Restaurant and I have to get it every time I'm in town. It's made with oat whiskey, Frangelico, and some house-made cherry syrup, maple whiskey, and brandied cherries.

Delicious.

Thanks to Michael Craig Beeck and Stacia Haase for the recipe and permission to share it.

Cheers!

Visit eatblackpig.com for more information on this fantastic restaurant.

Oat Fashioned

- 1.5oz Koval Oat Whiskey

- .5oz House Maple Whiskey

- .25oz Frangelico Hazelnut Liqueur

- .25oz House Luxardo Cherry Liqueur

- 2 Dashes Bitter Truth Orange Bitters

Instructions

1. Muddle Brandied Cherry, Orange, and 2 Dashes of Bitter Truth Orange Bitters in a standard old fashioned glass.

2. Add 1.5oz Koval Oat Whiskey, .25oz Maple Whiskey, .25oz Frangelico, and a Bar Spoon Luxardo Cherry Liqueur. Add Ice, Top with Club Soda, Give a Gentle Stir, and Garnish.

3. Garnish with Bacon and 1 Luxardo Cherry.

Brandied Cherries Recipe

1. Empty 12oz Cherry Jar of Juice - Set aside and use for other beverages.

2. Add your choice of brandy, being sure to cover cherries fully, and add 1 cinnamon stick.

3. Let sit for 24hrs before use.

House Maple Whiskey Recipe

1. Combine equal parts local Maple Syrup and your favorite whiskey.

2. Let sit for 24hrs to infuse.

3. Here, we combine 375ml Pure Wisconsin Maple Syrup with 750ml Larceny Bourbon Whiskey.

House Luxardo Cherry Syrup Recipe

1. Waste not, want not. A recipe to use the Luxardo cherry juice after all cherries have been used for garnish.

2. Ratio 2:1 - 1 cup Tito's Vodka and .5cup Luxardo Cherry Syrup.

3. Combine and let sit for 24hrs before use.

Author Note

I didn't plan to write this book. Alex Paige had other ideas.

Ever since I wrote the first scene in *Chaos in the Canyon*, I knew the next book would be centered around William's and Billy's wedding. I also knew Ben would be the victim. What I didn't know was that I needed to write this book right away.

I'd planned to begin writing another series after finishing Chaos, but during my morning writing session on September 1, this story began with my favorite first line I've written (to this point). From there, it flowed. And then stopped. And then reversed. And flowed again.

Writing fiction is weird.

I had to take a break from writing in October because I was teaching a writing workshop in Sheboygan. There, I serendipitously met Russ Green, the superintendent of the Wisconsin Shipwreck Coast National Marine Sanctuary. I asked him about a few plot points I had in mind, and he told me that yes, they were plausible.

Whew!

I still had questions, though. Specifically, could a 1,000-year-old dugout canoe be preserved at the bottom of Lake Michigan? Later that month, on my way home from an author conference in Chapel Hill, North Carolina, I stopped at Pilot Mountain State Park. My dad had mentioned the park and I thought, why not?

Inside the visitor center, hanging on the wall, was a 1,000-year-old dugout canoe that had been found in a river in Georgia.

Basically, I may not have planned to, but I was supposed to write this book when I did.

So what's real and what isn't? As you've probably guessed, the marine sanctuary is real. There are {X} shipwrecks inscribed in the National Register of Historic Places, and one of those is the S.S. Senator. When it and the {X} rammed into each other, the Senator was ferrying 256 Nash automobiles, and their "watery grave" is one of those protected shipwrecks.

It's also resting around 430 {x} feet under the surface, making it impossible to reach except by Remote Operated Vehicle. As far as I know, there have been no thefts from any of the shipwrecks.

What about the dugout canoe? My visit to Pilot Mountain confirmed one could be preserved for that long, and since the water in Lake Michigan is colder, it would be in much better shape than the one I saw. Those Indian Mounds are real, too, and they really were saved by a Garden Club.

Interestingly, earlier this week (as I write this) I visited Greenville, South Carolina for a quick lunch and a stroll along the river. A waymarking sign in {X} Park credited another garden club with saving the falls and creating the beautiful park. Who knew?

Who knew? has been my Sheboygan theme ever since I visited for the first time in 2021 and saw a t-shirt with the phrase. It quickly became one of my favorite destinations, and that was definitely influenced by the sailing lessons I took—and yes, I at first I *did* think I was going to kill my friend, our instructor, and myself, and the instructor assured me I couldn't because of the 900lb keel. It was also influenced by the John Michael Kohler Arts Center and the Kohler Arts Preserve, and by the city's impressive dining scene. The Oat Fashioned they drank is from Black Pig - recipe's in the back.

Also real is the Blue Harbor Resort. Alex prefers the first floor so she can walk right outside. Personally, I like being on the third floor so I can have my morning coffee on the balcony while watching the sun rise.

Sheboygan also has a book-themed garden, aptly named Bookworm Gardens. It's a charming, delightful place that really is fun for all ages.

What's not real? The yacht club, for one. While there is one, it doesn't look anything like the one I've created. I took some liberties with the marina, although the squat red lighthouse at the end of the breakwater is real.

This book is unusual for this series because most of the places exist. When something bad happens, I create the setting instead of placing it in an actual location. However, since Ben died on the breakwater and wasn't actually murdered, I figured it was fine to use a real spot.

The first time I visited Sheboygan at the end of August 2021, Alex hadn't been "born" yet. It would be another two months before she sprung out of my head. I had no idea that three years later, almost to the day, she'd insist on telling me a story, a story about standing up for what's right, standing up for yourself, and the power of knowing your own strength.

Who knew?

Acknowledgments

The setting in Alex Paige's books is always one of the characters. It helps define the tone of the story, its characters, and the overall feel.

That is definitely the case with this book.

My first thank you goes to Lori Helke. Lori's a fellow travel writer who lives in a small town near Sheboygan, and she frequently posted about how great the area was. My first press trip after completing breast cancer treatment was to Door County, Wisconsin, and since Sheboygan was on the way, I asked Lori if she could connect me with someone from Visit Sheboygan.

She did, and what joy that simple request has brought to my life.

That's where I met Shelly Harms, who quickly became one of my favorite people. That first weekend, Lori joined me for a day for sailing and eating, shopping and eating, visiting a brewery and eating, until we finished up with a slumber party in my room overlooking Lake Michigan.

Thank you, Lori and Shelly, for not only introducing me to your home, but for also becoming such dear friends.

Thanks also to Russ Green, who let me know my crazy ideas about bringing Nash autos to the surface could actually work, and other questions I had about the sanctuary.

I also want to thank SAIL, {Sheboygan sailing school}, for show-ing me the ropes and convincing me that Lori and I were perfectly safe on that teeny tiny boat, even with me steering the darn thing.

And thanks to my dad for suggesting I visit Pilot Mountain State Park. If you hadn't, I probably wouldn't have taken the time to stop there on my way back home. Because I did, I knew for a fact another one of my crazy ideas was plausible. And I also knew I had to write this book, right now. Serendipity!

Thanks also to Dad and to Mom for being my alpha readers, my editors, my sounding boards, my cheerleaders. It is so fun to have you two in my corner. It's also hard because you don't hold anything back, but I wouldn't have it any other way. So many of my scenes (especially those with police procedures) are stronger because of you.

Heidi Kohz—kisses and love and gratitude for buffing my unpol-ished manuscript and making it shine. I promise that next time I'll run it through my spelling and grammar checker first! Love you forever, soul sister.

Tatiana Abramova, editor extraordinaire—I *still* hear your voice in my head. Always will. You are amazing.

To all those who order my books while I'm still writing them, thank you! You lift me up and definitely contribute to keeping me on deadline. And hey—this time, I made it! Shelly Harms, Sherri Lieberman, Karen Gill, Henri Goudsmit, Sylvia Key, and so many others, your trust in me and your support keeps a smile on my face and my fingers on the keyboard.

And to you, dear reader. Thank you for loving to read, loving stories, and, hopefully, loving Alex Paige.

Where will she go next?

Also By Theresa L. Carter

As Theresa L. Carter

Alex Paige Books 1-5
Get the first five Alex Paige adventures!
Peril on the Peninsula
Revenge in the Rockies
Betrayed at the Beach
Ruin on the River
Chaos in the Canyon
Menace at the Marina

As Theresa L. Goodrich

Two Lane Gems, Vol. 1
Turkeys are Jerks and Other Observations from an American Road Trip
Two Lane Gems, Vol. 2
Bison are Giant and Other Observations from an American Road Trip
Living Landmarks of Chicago
Planning Your Perfect Road Trip

THERESA L. CARTER

Show Me Shipshewana
A Guide to Indiana Amish Country
Discover Geary County, Kansas
Nature, History, and Hometown Hospitality in the Sunflower
State

Publisher / Contributor

Midwest Road Trip Adventures, 2nd Edition
Midwest State Park Adventures

About Theresa L. Carter

Theresa's one of those voracious readers who grew up with her nose in a book and the desire to write her own. That took some time, as she spent years telling people where to go as a full-time travel writer before making it happen when she was 47 (because you're never too old to start). That book, *Turkeys are Jerks and Other Observations from an American Road Trip*, lit a long-dormant fire, and she's continued to write and publish travel books at a rapid pace ever since. She still wanted to write novels, though, and after a breast cancer gut punch, decided at age 51 not to wait any more. Alex Paige sprung out of her head, Athena-like, and hasn't left her alone since.

When Theresa's not telling people where to go or being told by Alex and friends what to write, she's reading (of course), learning, cooking, figuring out how to spend as much time outside as possible, or annoying her husband.

And sometimes, all of the above.

You can find Theresa on social media @theresastoryteller and at theresasbooks.com